Kingdom and Thrones: Lost in Zamarirria

by

RainbowPrince

Kingdom and Thrones: Lost in Zamarirria

Contact Information: info@thewildrosepress.com

Cover Art by *Debbie Taylor*

The Wild Rose Press, Inc.
PO Box 708
Adams Basin, NY 14410-0708
Visit us at www.thewildrosepress.com

Publishing History
First Edition, 2023
Trade Paperback ISBN 978-1-5092-4774-5
Digital ISBN 978-1-5092-4775-2

Published in the United States of America
Previously published on Amazon

In a book series called, Zae & Zuella "Kingdom & Thrones", Book One, you will encounter a lost individual called "Zae' ' who had been held against her will at the Kingdom of Reyvanne. She was being tortured by the guards there, bought fought her way through it, running through the Kingdom dodging all the guards plugging her way through their Kingdom while bleeding with open lacerations, and being fatigue, she made her way out and a search party was disbursed in capturing Zae again to put her to death. Struggling to make her way out to any safety, Zae kept going until she could no longer go any further. Found in the desert by the people of Zamairria, who is ruled by Goddess Zuella, Zae awakes in the kingdom, where she encounters Zuella for the first time. Zae is in a trance of being lost and having horror visions. But during her time in Zamairria, she is introduced to greater light, love and kindness of all that is known in the Kingdom of Zamairria. Zae is healing in this kingdom, where she falls in love with the Goddess Zuella. Throughout the book, you will find that other dark kingdoms are introduced and are somehow affiliated with Zae's mother who once ruled the kingdom of darkness and light.

During Zae's journey of finding out who she is, she will encounter many different and amazing creatures from the heavens and earth.

Chapter 1

Sheer Curtains in the Desert

Awoken during scorching heat, drenched from head to toe! Covered with pool of water across my body. I suddenly, realized this is quite bizarre, not recognize my surroundings, feeling a bit in a daze. The heat extremely burning with no breeze of air. I concluded, where can I possibly be at this time. I recognize where I was laying was on a flushed fine mat, made of palm leaves, strategically made. While noticing the quality of product used to make this mat. My mind realized, I was in a beautiful made tent, like desert tents, white sheer curtains blowing about with extreme hot air, pervasively sweating, unable to get cool, I began to get up catching my footing and as I was trying with effort to get up, suddenly an overwhelming feeling of dizziness took over and immediately I had to lay back down, I look around no one anywhere in site, but can hear soft spoken voices outside the tent. I gradually lay down and drug myself towards an opening of the tent which gave me a slight view of outside. I realized immediately that I have no clue who these people outside were, wrapped with cloches from their head to toe. Suddenly I felt fear of the unknown.

I heard male and female voices, seen what I would believe to be a female, wrapped in all white garment covered with gold sash covering her mouth. She looked at the tent where I believe then I was being held captive. This woman was quite tall, with piercing eyes, and a diamond in the middle of her forehead. She glances and our eyes caught each other, and she immediately looked away. But in matter of moments, looked back, as I open the curtain a bit wider, we just starred at one another as if we wanted to say something. I was wanting for this being to uncover herself so that I may look upon her, but suddenly people gathered quickly, and I went to laying back down. I hear entrance into the tent that I was in, male voices in a language that was like middle eastern. I made them believe that I was still asleep. There were two male voices I heard, I felt fear for their voices got loud and suddenly they left. Relieved of the unknown, fearful and perpetual overwhelming need of seeking anyone who speaks English.

I begin to turn to my right side and felt a pain that was quite excruciating, not noticing that I had been bandaged up with blood stains seeping through the cloth. Now I realized, I am somewhere, but nowhere to be found. Again, I heard voices near the tent and quickly lied back as if I were asleep. The voices were getting closer to the tent, but this time the voices were softer, they were female voices. My emotions of fear subsided knowing that the voices were females. There were four women, dressed in dark covered shawls and black sashes that covered their mouths, but as I peeked to my left side, there stands the same female that was outside the tent.

I couldn't bare not to wake up for I felt an immediate connection to this being. So, I began to wake up, anxiously wanting to let this being in white see me so that in hopes she would stay. I had gotten my wish; all the women left the room except her and another. She appeared to be someone of high status, but never said a word. The other woman attended to my wound, as the piercing eyed being just sat on a beautifully made chair just watching. I felt as if this being cared for me, but maybe I was in an illusion, since I was injured. I could barely come to light, then I had seen this being clap her hands once and suddenly males and females entered the tent. They all bowed down to her and I was completely in awe. Wow! Who is this beautiful being? They spoke to her, but the other woman, answered for this being. She was very mysterious I thought. I was dying to have her unveil herself. But she said something to a servant lady, matter of seconds, individuals were coming in and out of the tent bringing trays of food, cuisines, fruits, and cups made with gold, and beautiful wrapped gems. The people had brought in tables made of red oak, seemingly hand crafted and just shined with varnish to glaze across the wood giving it such a vibrant look. The dinner ware made of gold.

As I got up, I noticed they have made only two seating's, and seated me on one end and this beautiful being at the other. The food and all drinks were made efficient to a dinner for the upmost high. This beautiful being then clapped twice and suddenly the tent was empty, and I found myself there with this beautiful being and all this food, wine and fruit. She made a hand gesture to me as if I should eat, then I reach out to a platter of lamb and put some on my plate to eat. I found my appetite to be quite hungry. I was eating, drinking and this beautiful being just watched me.

So, I asked, "Will you not eat with me?". She then reached for her sash to remove it gradually, and to my surprise, she was radiantly exquisite. Never seen this type of beauty! She was amazingly gorgeous, I believe she said "Eat", but I was so mesmerized by her captivating beauty that I just stuck the meat in my mouth and forgot to bite. At this time, I believe she finally uttered the words, "How do you feel?" I said in my head! "Omg, she speaks English. I am about to get to know this beautiful being to". She had a way about her beautiful brown piercing eyes, dimples on both of her cheeks, graciously full lips, and sensual cleft on her chin. Embarrassed by my table etiquette, I apologized, I felt as if I haven't eaten for days. She then stated "My people found you by the water where the camels seem to herd at times, so they brought you here. You have been sleeping for two days". She said, "I had them attend to your wounds, but I checked on you to make sure your condition was getting better". I then told her "I don't remember anything or how I ended up in this place. I don't even recall my name". She then looked down and stated, "Eat up and I will have them get a bath ready for you". I asked her, are you leaving, and she said, "Why are you ok?" I then mentioned I prefer she stays, for some reason, I felt as if I were safe with her presence. She then looked up and took a bite from strawberry and said, "I will stay!" I was relieved.

Chapter 2

Kingdom of Zamairria

We concluded dining, and again she clapped once, a few women came and gathered everything to clean up. While cleaning men brought in a beautifully bronze tub shape in a form of a shell, while filling it with hot water, and some type of soap lathering in suds of soap bubbles. Then others were bringing towels, little fragrant bottles, and leaving them on table. I sat there, thinking to myself, "I know this bath is for me, but I'd be damned to take a wash in front of these people". Suddenly all disbursed out except the beautiful being and the one lady who seemed to be her helper. She rarely said much, but the lady tended to my wound helping me to unwrap and when she did this, the beautiful being, said something in different language and suddenly she left. This left me alone with this being! She sat down tilted her head down and put her sash back on, while I started to undress for the bath. She did not say a word, awkward moment. But it did not seem to bother me at any point.

I felt as if she was watching me, so I continued to undress and stepped into the tub. The bath was so warm, but mind you it was scorching hot air outside, so I was hoping the water to be cool. I then told this beautiful being, "How is it that the water should be hot, in this weather so fiery hot". She then replied, "It helps clean, so that any infection will be killed immediately". She then said, "It will be okay!" I trusted her, although the water was immensely hot. She said, "Do you not know where you are from?" I stated "I cannot recollect anything. My name, I don't even know where I live.

If I've even had a family". I then asked, "Where am I?" She said "You are at the Kingdom of Zamairria, I am Goddess of light. We are of a different world. Here in our world, women are the sole key to empowering the culture. We are held in the utmost regard". I said to her, "Then who are you? Why is it that everyone seems to abide in how you clap?" She then replied, "You need not know of what matters are dealt with here and how? All I can tell you is that you should not worry, and no harm will come to you". I sighed with relief but at the same time, could not help but wondered what has happened and where do I belong? Why do I feel this Goddess has a gentle but strong spirit? I asked, "How long you will be here and what are you guys going to do with me?". She said, "After your bath, we will head to the palace". Then two women came back into the tent, and guided the Goddess out, and I got up out of the tub grabbed a towel and said, "Stop what is your name? Where are you going?" and then the curtains closed with me being left alone in the tent. I quickly got dressed in clothes that were left on the side table.

I found myself urgently getting dressed in garments that I was unfamiliar with. But hence forth, I surged to the curtain and opened it. The Goddess was nowhere to be seen. Appeared before me were the two ladies that helped me before, one speaking to me in English and said, "We will be outside your tent and if there should be anything you if need one of us, we would be always at your call". I then went back into the tent. I thought to ask the women where the Goddess has gone off too! But did not quite get the nerve to ask. I went back in seeing a sofa type bed on the side of the tent. Noticing that this tent seemed to be very large. Why hadn't I noticed this before. But to my surprise, there was a knock on the wooden part of the tent where the tent opens, and two men came through stating if I am ready. I said ready, "for what?". They one said, "Come with us". I follow them needing help because I was still kind of lightheaded, so one of the men said to the female outside my tent, "Help her". The women both help me into a somewhat beautiful glass looking carriage, it was pulled with two white stallions, and the coach was all so lovely. It had a steep temple golden colored top, carved ever so clearly with what appeared to be the Goddesses head sculpted into it.

Then off we went, and I had no idea where this was heading. But as one of the ladies pull back a sheer curtain, I can see nothing but the mirage of the heat from all the sand, it was golden brown, this bristle of sand had a yellowish red vibrant gleam to it. It was awfully hot yet so beautiful. We road into the deepest desert it appeared to be. But within a 45 min ride, I notice palm tree half a mile apart and in front looked as if I see a pool of water. There were more than a dozen palms, separated apart. But as we got in closer it seemed as if we were going to enter an underground compound built under the hills of the desert. We came to an entrance that was covered as if curtains were hanging, I wondered what lie beyond these curtains, it was not an average tent, it was a size of a kingdom.

The carriage stopped in front while three men pulled the curtain panel back, and another three on other end.

Noticing the doors made up of crystals 40 ft. High and 25 ft wide. It looked as the crystals imbedded in the doors was so much brighter and crystalized by the essence of the sun shining so bright unto the doors. It took two men to open each side, and as the doors open, my mouth drop in awe of how the compound of this kingdom was even created. Realizing it was not a dream, I pinched myself, I could not believe my eyes. From where the door entrance opens, I could see clearly the chairs that were straight ahead from me. The chairs were of two bronze, two silver, two gold, and one illuminating type looking chair. The Goddess was sitting there. There were quite a few people surrounding the compound so beautifully designed of carvings of images, crystalized glasses, tables made of maple wood with the most elegant hand carving. Fruit bowls, made of oak wood, plates of gold on tables, silver ware beyond crystals, everything seemed to be crystalized lighting, beautiful carving with wood, golden artifacts of images just beautiful flowers, plants colorful never seen before. The aroma lingered in the air of such lovely, sweet scent, fresh. I am still standing at the foot of the entrance, overwhelmed of the beauty. Then the Goddess claps again once, and the two women guide me down the aisle.

Chapter 3

Goddess Zuella

Walking alongside, I see the high ceilings beautiful images carved into the crystalized material that was built. The light of the sun beam right above, giving the illumination through its crystalized look above. Still making my way down to the Goddess, I was noticing all such beauty that was in the compound, and the females wore eggshell and brown cloches, with matching sashes, there were children dancing about and laughing, singing welcoming me and waving. As I started to walk forward, I finally reached the front where two male individuals wearing gold garments with crowns, two females wearing silver with some sort of exquisite design bands worn around their hair, the other two males were wearing what appeared to be bronze armor, with swords hung at their side designed in a very peculiar manner, but amazing.

Then after noticing these individuals, I turned to my left, where I had seen the Goddess stand out of what was considered her chair of glacier clear sparkle imbedded into the glass. Her hair colored was fiery red hot, texture of the curls in her long scribed as the curves and edges which break in a current. Her hair vibrations red, one deeper, then other lighter shade which enhances her hair where it appears to shine abundantly radiant. She has on her head, a crown elegant, sparkly, with a material I've not yet come across. It had her head shot circulating around, and in between torches of flames and vines around the crown. I believe there was flaming red diamonds running all around end to end top and bottom. Her hair was so fully laid out that her crown sat perfectly on her head. As she stood there, her gown was of a crystalize look just flickering of shine in every movement she made! There were multi- colors that gleamed, and her collar was raised halfway above the back of her head. It was four pointed edges on back with a cape cloche which connect to her collar but as she stood there two maid servants approach her from back to release her cloche then we were able to get a visual exactly what this beautiful being was wearing. Her skin tone was ever so illumination with a touch fair golden crème color with speckles of multi- color hints contrasting within her skin. Her gown was amazing, the garment hugged her torso fitted her eloquently sheered eggshell color fit as a mermaid within her fitted shell scale suit.

Covering her waistline, a material matching her crown, the garment was not one to be seen ever, she was fascinating. The garment had lighted silky looking material but clear, the material apparently looked clear not revealing any of her parts of her body except her shoulders. She looked smashing, out of this world. Illuminating as she stands as if the light befell on her directly. I starred at her as if I saw her for the first time, because all I can recollect is the very first time that our eyes caught standing outside of the tent.

Her eyes were as piercing as right now while I look upon her. She had such an eloquent gown, grabbed her torso, being able to see her fit as well as flare as the gown started by her hips, as if there were layers of material but rather sheen a lighted clothe, looking as it were see through but not being able to see her skin. It was crystalized with many sequences, diamond gems but fiery red gems crystals aligned throughout her entire dress. From front to back, running alongside were just beautiful designs of a goddess imbedded in the material. This beautiful being finally spoke and said, to the people sitting to her side to welcome me. They all stood up and two servant maid women came to the front of me with a beautifully made cloche, that appear to be the brightest looking chrome colored garment, engaged with deep black obsidian gems place into the garment as if it were made to fit a prince. These two women then approached with the garment placed out to put over my shoulder!

I felt so honored, but was not sure how to react, but just bowed my head and say thank you. A second later there was a chair which was brought out for me to sit in. This chair had a piercing black color which had a shape of an individual's head, but the face was left in an image where you could not see exactly the face of the carving in this chair. It was beautifully made with chrome color diamonds instill alongside the arm of the chair. At the top was a design of a prince crown carved into the chair. I was not knowing should I sit, or how to react of all the effortless kindness that was being bestowed upon me. During all this while, I was just trying to take in what was happening, I could not help but think, what is happening? These people are so kind, there is not one blemish of ill feelings in this entire palace. Throughout the whole place, every being seemed to be filled with lighted, welcoming peace. I then took the offer of taking a seat, there was an immediate surge of peace that overtook my emotions.

Rather than questioning, I suddenly was not looking for any answers, but just the feeling of complete joy and peace came to me. Everyone surrounding me as well as this beautiful being took their seats. She then looks directly at me and stated, "Welcome to the Kingdom of Zamairria. I am Goddess Zuella, the keeper of the people. To my left sits the two men in bronze who protect the beings of this palace as well as our allies. The two women who sit in the silver, are my wise counsels. The other two men that are in gold, are the sole key of how the peace is maintained throughout our Kingdom. We are a kingdom hidden within a desert. We can only be seen by those who hold elements of higher light and peace. We are a kingdom, that no harm befalls. There are various other kingdoms that exist outside our palace. There are children of the trees, our sand screens, our flying stallions who guard the air and others, who are under our kingdom but have their sole reason for existence. There is a darkness that scatters throughout the outer walls of our palace, that over 100's of years, we have not yet to come to face them but hear multiple stories of how brutal, dark, and relentless these beings live".

"Then are heard to be none lighted, with securing their kingdom through all cost. They take no heed to for the humble but lead with arrogance and destruction. This kingdom is Wisteria, ruled by a king, who is King Waes, and his wife Queen Welza, and two daughters Weezia and Waazrie. The family is known for their cruelty, judgmental and arrogance. The two princesses are of direct blood line to the King and Queen, but there has been talk of one of the princesses, to have a softer side then all. We are not sure, but there has been some talk of this princes at times.

We have existed hundreds of years and always been lighted. But there has been an uproar lately about the troubles in the Kingdom of Wisterria. There is one other kingdom called Reyvane, this is a place where many have free will to choose whether to do good or not! This kingdom is ruled by King Rezzem, whom has a daughter named Zae and son named Raz. His Queen Resenti, was murdered but up till today have never been known to who had killed his Queen. As the time proceeds and years have passed, multitudes have been crying in these two kingdoms for peace and righteousness. It has come to my attention many of times, to pursue the light within these two kingdoms, but I have stood still in hopes that these two will have arrive to their senses and chose the better and live with light then to kill one another, hence for the darkness that prevails itself into their kingdom".

Chapter 4

Flashes of Horror

During the time of the explanations of Zuella, my mind seemed to have flashes of scenes that were quite startling. I stood as if nothing had bothered me but was quite intrigued of the tales that were being told by Goddess Zuella. As she then finalized the surroundings of the world, a sudden mirage of what came to mind was very disturbing. There was a flash of gruesome, killings of how people were beheaded, beaten and sent to dungeons. There I stood with a quite look as if were puzzled, then I shook my head to try and pay attention to what was going on.

I then came to my senses realizing that it probably was just images of darkness trying to overtake my mind. The light that shined in the palace where I stood. Allowed me to feel as if they were just images and that I was able to shake it off. Minutes later there was music played from not of any that I ever heard before, so much peace in just hearing it. Then within matter of seconds there came all these women wearing cloches covering their faces, if I were to count, I would say about twelve. They were all caring large trays of silver filled with a feast of food, meats, vegetables, fruits and wine glasses.

Six men followed behind the women, with large pouches over hanging on their arms filling our glasses with wine. But it all seemed to perfect. I kept having these destructive thoughts that were trying to enter my mind, leaving me to shake my head, trying to get rid of these flashes that were trying to haunt me. Anyhow it appeared as if it were a feast, but this feast was unimaginable, simply out of the realm that I have never encountered before in my lifetime. Back to what was taking place in the beautiful palace in where I stood. There was absolutely no type of darkness surrounding anyone or anything within the kingdom, the only darkness that tried to make its way in was only in my mind.

Goddess Zuella then stood, she looked right at me and said, "Enjoy! lets feast to celebrate the light that will soon be of one accord across the world. Light is the sole key of the evolution of Kingdom of Zamairria. We will teach all good nature, kindness and Love, throughout all beings. I hereby announce that, the Kingdom of Zamairria, will triumph over darkness that is imbedded of other kingdoms". Then I ate, drank and enjoyed myself to the fullest listening to the beautiful music in background being played. Although I found myself having such a gratifying time like never. I was moved in areas in my mind that I could not fathom of the peace felt within the palace. It apparently seemed to be that this world was completely, utterly untouched with any type of dark.

Those feelings of destruction, anger, and danger were nowhere to be found in the kingdom. No pain existed from here at all. It's almost as if I truly believed that I belonged to this world permanently. I still was feeling a bit lightheaded, then Zuella pointed out if there was anything that I would need, I quickly replied, if she would be so kind to excuse me if I could be taken somewhere to lie down, for I felt a bit woozy, she then looked at me with a glare in her eyes and stated "Your wish will be honored". As she was speaking, I looked upon her and stated, "Will you be by" I don't know whether that was an appropriate question to ask her, knowing of her status. But she simply covered her face and then looked down without a word. She then clapped again once, and her maidservants approached me to help me up then guided me to where I was to lay my head and rest. I just could not believe the halls and the entirety of the palace, was so elusive, elegant, and heavenly according to how I can possibly describe, my words do no justice of the amazing the entire surrounding then I was taken to a room in the palace where the outer doors, where made of crystals imbedded with fiery red stones, with a crown of prince carved at the tip of the doors, colored in chrome. As one of the women to the handle to open the door, they opened slightly and to my surprise, the room was magnificently made. A bed made of dazzling chrome, built for a king.

Huge mantle with illuminating candles burning throughout room, plus fireplace burning dim, and most elegant fragrant scent. I was feeling a bit dizzy at the time. I was helped into the bed, then the maidservants left me to rest in the room. I sat up in bed and took another look around. The room was breathtaking, as if everything in the palace. I could not stop being in awe, of the exquisite beauty that surrounded me. There were also vases filled with beautiful looking flowers as well as peacock feathers, and a glacier looking tub. It was so fascinating and sexy look all together. I then laid down on a bed so cozy, pillows that were so soft, fluffy, and beyond comfortable, that my head just sunk in, and I believe I passed out. During the time that I knocked out, I believe I saw the most elusive things probably that could not be even fathom in a lighted beings mind. The truth of it all is that I tossed and turned and was in a heap of pool of water when I woke suddenly with fear of the dreams that were occurring throughout my mind. There were such evil acts, of killing and deaths, pure ravish of hatred, worse than animals fighting each other in vicious ways. I could not stop awakening, because of the dreams. Leaving me in a pool of sweat! Each time I awoke, I felt a bit fearful, but the overpowering of light helped me to come at ease. Although I was having these dreams the face of Goddess Zuella, would appear multiple times in my mind. The visions of her in my mind, helped ease the dreams. I felt at times a warmth comforted feeling. As if she were there with me in my dreams.

Chapter 5

Unforbidden Touch

I was suddenly awoken by breaking of glass, I sat up and looked around and found a person covered with a silk light cloche covering head to toe, then quickly we caught eyes, but a totally different type of stare to the Goddess. This individual almost seem to be very suspicious. I then looked on floor and there appeared to be a vase cracked, shattered glass all over floor, with peacock feathers and flowers. This individual dashed out quickly from the room. Not knowing what went on, I was a bit confused on what just happened, I just starred at the dim light that the fireplace was lighting. During this time, I was still having memories with flashes of horror.

It almost appeared as if a half hour had passed by, and I found myself dazing off! I then awoke, by the sound of someone entering the room I was sleeping in. This time, I just lied there and peeked with one eye open to see if it were that individual again. To my surprise, it appeared to be a maidservant as well as Goddess Zuella. I then slightly got up and asked Zuella, "Hello your highness!" She stated, "We stopped by to see if there was anything you need". I asked her to take a seat let's talk a bit. She said something to her maidservant, and a second later we were alone. I told her "Thank you so much for her kindness". I also stated, "Do you have any family, children, or are you married?" She was very quiet for minutes. I then asked her if she was not comfortable speaking to me, then pardon my manners. She looked up, then slowly uncovered her mask. I started to get up making my way to the edge of the bed. I began to get off the bed walking around the room, still conversing with the Goddess. At one point I bent over to pick up a peacock feather lying on the floor. We talked about the Kingdom of Zamairria, and her part in the ruling of her world. I felt a bit dizzy and went back to sit on bed. I almost passed out and lost my footing, but Goddess Zuella, quickly got up to come to my aide. I grabbed her to catch my footing. Then we just stared into each other's eyes, couldn't tell how long we stared at each other, she then pulled back and I took her hand and said, "Please remove your mask". She just looked at me, then slowly removed her mask for me.

I then looked at her, without saying a word I reached up and brought her close to me to sit beside me. Then I took her hand and she was reluctant at first, but then she just let me hold her hand. I was just mesmerized by the glowing of her radiance. Her beauty is lovely, and so unbelievably gorgeous. We looked at each other for minutes without no words spoken. I then took my right hand to put up by her face, then gracefully stroked her slightly on the left cheek, not knowing what is happening between us at this moment. But it appeared as if we were just knowing something intensifying between us was at its birth. I then moved closely within five inches from Goddess Zuella face, she did not move away. I then pulled her head closer, still not knowing these emotions that we were tugging with apparently. That precise moment, I then moved in towards her lips, I moved in and gradually moved my head in to kiss her. Without hesitation, Zuella then kissed back and before you know it the kiss began to be passionate, that grew into intensifying. We probably were locked in our kissing motion, somewhere between 10minutes if I were to guess. It was mesmerizing to a degree of illusion that is greatly felt. Suddenly a great bang hit the doors, and we both stopped kissing immediately, became quiet. Goddess Zuella, immediately got up off the bed and went right back to sitting on her chair. She then spoke a language I was unfamiliar with. It apparently seems as if there was an urgency to the knock. So, at that time 2 maidservants and 4 armored men walked into the bedroom. The one armored guy, wearing all black with blue sash stated something in the language that Goddess was speaking and then the women came to the side of Goddess and helped her out of the seat. They all left with a state of urgency, leaving me in the room by myself again. Wondering what just happened to me and the Goddess put me in a state of mind of feelings of over joy as well as suspense of what happened to have the Goddess leave suddenly. Within minutes, two women entered my room without knocking and I asked where the Goddess had gone, but they replied we came to get you ready! I then said, gladly allow me to get myself ready.

The two women then went out the door and stated they will be waiting outside for me, so that when I am done, just come out of the door and they will take me to where I am to go! I then quickly got changed, and went with the women, whom then took me within the palace halls, leading me to an underground passage which lead to a podium lit by the shine from the sun that was above.

It was made of crystal glass which pulled back as a scroll leaving the top opening as if there were gliding glasses to pull back. I then looked carefully, shaking my head at what lie straight in front of my eyes. It appeared to be a white stallion with wings.

I stood there again and pinched myself shaking my head as if I were in an amazing dream where this had to be an illusion. I then asked the two women what is going on and what is that which I am looking at in front of me! They said this is not a dream, we have to get you to where Goddess is heading since they have had a head start the only way to get you there on time to meet her would be to utilize, Lightening, (the white wing stallion) whom is her personal flying being. I'm completely delusional currently, saying to myself "there is no way in hell I'm getting on that!" One of the women, then said that is the only way to get to Zuella, without taking days. Lightening is very friendly, and she feels people's spirit, if you were of bad karma, she would have quickly then picked up before you can get within 5ft of her. The lady said, go up and pat her to see if you take to her, because apparently, she takes to you! So, I did exactly that, and walked my way up slowly to Lightening, and to my surprise she just looked at me as I raised my hand to pat her. The stallion seemed to take to me, at this time I was trying to take in what all is going on, so I told one of the women, "what is it for me to do?" She then said, get on! So, I did, and Lightening made me so comfortable. I then held on tight while she glided me into the air. This was quite the most illuminating thing that I have ever experienced in my entire life. This ride into the air, with a horse with wings, is completely unthought of, nor reality. But today, it is mine, I'm flying with a beautiful white stallion in the skies, the view from up here as well as the ride, was breathtaking. I can see, the whole entire desert sand, palm trees gathered in a remote area. It was like a world outside of the palace that appeared to be serene. As I looked all around, I look to my left, which was west I could see the palm trees gathered in multitudes, and the ocean which was far out shadowing the palms in the desert. Unto my right to the east, it had mirage images of sandcastles built as if they were villages. The bright shine from the sun seemed to grab the golden bristles of sand falling on ground, making it shimmer. I then look straight ahead viewing the north where, it seemed to have mountains of peaks rich green, and what to appear to be waterfalls in a crystal light form. Then I look towards my back, which would be south, I see a dark covered sky that just looks dim, no light as if it were a world clouded with dark shadow. I suddenly felt an eerie feeling come over me as I starred towards the south. I quickly then looked back to get away from that feeling. In noticing that Lightening was headed towards the east. I kind of felt at ease, knowing we were not headed the way where the clouds were. The journey in the air was amazing, but in my mind, I kept wondering where is Goddess Zuella, and why did she have to leave the Kingdom of Zamairria, to come out into this world that had feelings of darkness. Her Kingdom is so illuminating with goodness, light, beautiful aura and uplifting spiritual love, that I did not understand the trip Goddess would have made outside of her own palace. As Lightening, began to fly lower, I almost fell off by the surprise of the horse's voice, stating, we are almost there! I nearly died, of surprise, a horse with wings, not only that but talked. No, this is quite my mind playing some sort of tricks on me for sure. We got closer, then I said to the horse, do you talk? Or is this all in my head! To my surprise again, the horse replied, we are almost there! I said, oh my goodness! This is out of my mind! Wow, I am not dreaming! This is outrageous, I can't believe this! As we approach the land for arrival, I then notice, multitudes of people gathering around. All these individuals were with garments covering from head to toe! All clothed for sand weather, although the scenery was enticing, it seemed immensely hot. But there was the carriage that was the same one that had picked me up from where they had founded me. It seems to be as everyone was cluttered around, as if there was something major going on. I then noticed the men in armor at my room. Lightening was probably 30ft in the air before we hit ground. So, I was able to catch a glimpse of what surrounded the area which we were about to land. Suddenly Lightening said, not to worry that I will be okay, and if I were needing to leave, she would be waiting for me. I was comforted by this notion offered by the white stallion. We were about to land in a few minutes as the crowd starred up to see us flying down. They were all in great surprise, plus you could hear them talking about! Not clearly making out what is being said! But I am just thankful, I guess I will be seeing Goddess Zuella soon! To my surprise, people started yelling and stating that is she! I'm looking all around, but their hands seem to have pointed up in the air towards my direction. I then knew they were just surprised as I was, regarding the flying stallion with wings. We then landed, before I could even come down from Lightening, I was ambushed and thrown onto the ground.

Chapter 6

Reyvane

Grabbed and drug across the ground. Lightening gallantly flew away! Probably fearing for what was happening to me! To my relief, I clearly heard a male voice, shout, "get back" then as I looked up, I seen the armored men at the room shoving people in the crowd off me! People were shouting, "murderer, that's her, get her" and angered with the notion to get me for some reason! Thank God, that the armor men showed up to help me! They then grabbed me up, to pick me up off the ground, and guided me to a place where there was like a coliseum

But built with pillars of carvings that were quite unusual, as I was taken into this place. There were a crowd of people throughout entire coliseum, but there was a room within there, that had a layer of beautiful red wood door. This room was as if there were filled with gold and silver artifacts. I walked in guided by two of armored men. They took me directly to the chair that was presented at the middle of the room. There was an individual with a mysterious type appearance. You could not quite tell their face because they had a steel mask on their face which hid their look. This person had a deep voice which carried and when spoken, grabbed everyone's attention. At this time, I noticed this person spoke the same language as I. But also, he turned to the armored men and spoke their tongue. I thought this to be of great surprise to me. This person seems to be asking about me, I would presume! But then again, I would be just taking a guess. This man behind the mask had a voice which trembles as if it were a voice compared to Gods. Though I had no idea what I was doing there, it appeared to be that Goddess Zuella was nowhere in sight. So, I just waited, till I had to be taken to a place in the colosseum, where there was talk in the language which I understood. This talk was about an individual which was murdered, killed just right outside the compound of the palace. Kingdom of Zamairria, there were people talking about how it had to be the sand screens. Which the people of Zamairria are there to defend their people whom they look over. Therefore, that explains the present of the armored men, and one of the individuals seated up front when I first was welcomed into the palace, (Kingdom of Zamairria). There were two counsels, and if I am not mistaken there appeared one of the individuals I noticed and recognized. But still not sure of what has taken place, I thought I were brought here to meet Goddess Zuella. It was obvious that she was nowhere to be found. The individual that I recognized as one of Goddess Zuella's protector of Zamairria, was conversing with this man behind mask. With the two armored men, beside him with me still seated in the chair, the conversation was subtle but at times got a bit rugged. This went on for 15-20 min. I was feeling tired, then I see the one individual which was one of Zuella's honored people who seated across from her went I walked into the palace. This person got up and was guided with helpers to his side. He then turned to the two armored men from Zamairria, and said something in their language, he then came by me and said, that he will see me at the palace of Zamairria. I then said, ok! But within seconds, he had left and the man behind the mask looked straight ahead, at the time the individual was leaving, as the doors shut I stood up on my own accord, thinking that it was time to go, but to my surprise as the doors shut, that same time two arrows shot straight into the forehead of the armored men that were from Zamairria, killing them instantly, these men were supposed to have taken me back to the palace. But to my surprise they were just assassinated, right before my eyes. Oh, my goodness, how are they supposed to know that I am here. Immediately, the man behind the mask, had his guards or soldiers come through, removing the bodies of the two armored men from Zamairria, and they grabbed me to pull me outside of the chair, with me saying what are you guys doing, where are you taking me! I demand to see Goddess Zuella. Then the people who appeared to serve the man behind the mask, took me to stand in front of the man with the mask. He then said, to me, "Do you know who I am?" I looked at him, and said, "What are you doing? You just murdered innocent men! Why and what made you do that?" He turns to me, then turns around leaving me to face his back. I heard his voice again, and for some reason it sounds familiar. He then says, "Do you not know who I am?" I stood there, with many flashes running through my mind of horror and for some apparent reason it seems to be familiar. Then I hear from the man with the mask, say "Zae, do you not know me yet?" As soon as the name Zae was uttered, I then recollected exactly who I am. Where I came from, as well as knowing that my mother was murdered Queen Resenti. Till this day my mother's murderer, never has come to light. Still not saying a word to the man in the mask, I did not say anything. I went on acting as if I don't know who he is, nor have any recollection of who I am. I then answered hysterically saying "Who is Zae? Where am I?" This man removed his mask, I then knew exactly who he is, but I still held my ground in acting as if I had no recollection of anything! He looked at me and said, 'What has happened, why do you not know who you are?" I then replied, "All I know is that you just had two men murdered right before my eyes." I knew exactly who this man was, he was married to my mother, he was known to be King of the Kingdom of Reyvane. His name is King Rezzem. I started to remember bits and pieces of things that were in my mind. But I made sure to not allow him nor anyone know that I started to gain my memory. But as this was happening, I feared for my life. The man with the mask then had me removed to a place where I had a room but locked up putting guards outside of my door making sure that I would not leave nor have anyone come in. They had me guarded, but now I was even more fearful the sole reason, remembering this man, gave me visions of how cruel he was to my mother and me.

Chapter 7

Search Party

Returning back to Zamairria, the individual, named Zeheeles, had spoken at the Kingdom of Reyvane, on behalf of the people of Zamairiria, had walked in to the palace, where Goddess Zuella had seated, with her notion of listening to the individual give his report of what went on over in Reyvane. But before he uttered anything else, Goddess Zuella, replied and said, "That they had killed our two armored men, (the protectors) and how was it that our guest was held captive over there? How did she get out of her room knowing that she was unable to travel far distance in her condition?" The man said, "How is it that you know these things, and why was she even taken there. Plus, before I had left there, I said to the young lady that we will see each other at the palace upon her return," she slightly turned and said, "Ok!" Before anything else was uttered, here comes in the Goddess Zuella's servant, helper, her right hand, named Zehiah. She has served to be Zuella's most loyal servant. Zuella then says to Zehiah, "What seems to be happening?" Zehiah, then replies, "The podium where Lightening stands fast awaiting is empty and she is gone." Then Goddess Zuella, says, "I am concerned for her safety but more so, the young lady that we had in our care is no longer here. Find out who let go, gather the protectors of Zamairria, and have them do what is needed to be done. I want someone to tell me the well being of the lady who was under our care. Find out where she is, and who she is, and if she is ok? Zehiah, let all my counsels be notified as well as the protectors of Zamairria be informed to meet with their counsels, restore all surrounding protection around the palace, and allow the packs of stallion to be alarmed to gather in search of Lightening and call them forward." All counsels of Zuella gathered as they were being directed for plans of searching for the young lady that was cared for at the Kingdom of Zamairria, as well the Stallion, which belongs to Goddess Zuella. Now Zuella, stands with an illuminating globe around her saying things in her language, where the dome of crystalized glass, colored with rainbow colors, that was directly above her head opened as it did, the sky shined with a radiant blue and deep magenta in it, with a yellowish, bright orange rays radiantly shining outward from the sun. There were stampedes of flying beings migrating in the sky which appeared to be the horses with wings. The horses were of all colors of the rainbows. If you were to count, there were at least hundreds, four of the horses flew right inside the palace, they were colored, red, yellow, orange, and blue. The people surrounding the Goddess, seem to be surprised. Then the Goddess stated that it has come time, for the people of Zamairria, to know whom their Goddess overseas, in means of caring and ruling. The mountains, water, all living creatures, and those who are truly lighted with no blemish are whom serve the Goddess, the Kingdom of Zamairria. So now everyone in Zamairria knows the existence of why we are here, plus hidden to those whom not of the light. People as well as the horses were disbursed and they all were gone, all horses flew into the sky with every lighted being, whom serves the Goddess. While the disbursing of the people in Zamairria, there were thousands that stayed behind with the Goddess to situate the palace and make sure that things were handled and kept in order. She then took her seat. Her highness was then approached minutes later after the disbursing of her followers to answer the demand of the Goddess. Zehiah, then walked up to Zuella, and whispered in hear ear. Zehiah said, "there has been an uproar outside the palace, as well as inside, about an incident that occurred behind the walls of Kingdom of Reyvane, with King Rezeem. There has been talk of the children of King Razeem, whom he had with his Queen, that murder which till today no one has found, plus the disappearance of one of his kids. They claim to have stated that his kids were put to death or killed somehow. But no one truly knows. Statements been made that there were two kids, one male and other female. Besides, there is lots of talk that the kids of King Rezeem, were not too fond of him and his tactics of his ruling."

Then Zehiah waited for the Goddess's to reply, Zuella, reached slightly over to Zehiah's ear and whispered something back, shortly after Zehiah, then walks away and was gone. Now at the palace, Kingdom of Zamairria, the people were scattered, busy getting things ready, preparing also the protection of Zamairria, and the Goddess counsels, ended up letting them seek out their right-hand individuals and delegated their duties to be excuted. There were knocks at the front of the palace doors, so Goddess Zuella, stated to her protectors, whom could possibly be knocking on our doors. The counsel man, named " Zehish" walked closer to the doors escorted by his guards, then open the doors of the palace of Zamairria, and to their surprise, was greeted by the children, who are known to be the tree children. There were just four kids, three boys and a girl! They stated they were there to see Goddess Zuella. Out of the four children, they all about 8 years old, they were not siblings but were known as the children of the tree. All four of them said, simultaneously, "Your highness, there was a person killed by the trees where the sand screens border from our land. One of the kids, seen who killed this person, but now the kid, named Yzelle, whom is a girl about 7 years old. We can not find her anywhere, we need help, Goddess Zuella. Can you please help us find her! We looked everywhere for her but have not been able to find her. We believe she is hiding somewhere, because she is scared. So, we gathered together to come here and seek help to find Yzelle". Goddess Zuella, said to her wise counsels, "Get all the children of the tree, and bring them back to the palace, they will be safe here at the Kingdom of Zamairria." "Although the kids, seem to be reluctant to find their way here, we came on behalf of the children of the tree. So please, Goddess Zuella, send help for us to find, Yzelle." Then Goddess, said "Need not to worry, we will find her. Now come and my people will feed you all and take care of you now."

Chapter 8

The Sand Screens

Back in the Kingdom of Reyvane, Zae was seeking diligently how to break free from where they were holding her captive. Although, King Razeem had guards put right outside her door, she remained cool, calm and collective. Zae was put in a room that was secured at the windows, as well as concrete walls, being one way in and one way out of the room where she was being held. In her mind, she was trying to remember ways to get out of there. But to her surprise, she realized that it would probably take some type of disturbance. All she had around her was candles burning, so she then thought to take a chance and wet a cloth, that was on the table in room and took the candle lit and started to burn the curtains in the room starting fires to anything that would burn, taking this big chance she then yelled to the guards out the door, "screaming fire, please help!" then the guards immediately open the door running in, and Zae took the bottom of the steel candle holder and hit one of the guards directly in back of his neck, knocking him out, and making her way, running as fast as she can, ending up through the halls of the coliseum, where there were crowds, of people about, she got lost there and made her way outside, asking an innocent bystander for her cloche. This individual gave her a fusia, and velvet garment and

Zae immediately covered her head, covering her body. There were guards disbursed throughout the coliseum, in search for Zae, whom had run off. Everywhere was full of people, guards grabbing people to look upon their faces. Zae made her way discretely outside of the compound of the coliseum, then started walking, in the meanwhile she kept getting memories of her surroundings. She came upon an area, which was two miles outside the coliseum. There was nothing but sand, as well as a great dip of loosely type puddles of sand appearing to be wet, or even a mirage of sand since the weather was extremely hot. By this time, there was no water to be found. Zae found herself to very fatigue. She then started to walk along and suddenly caught her foot in something that seem to grab her and begin sucking her into the ground. Knowing that there was no one in sight, she didn't even start yelling. As she was halfway into the ground, she realizes that there was no help and she is going to die. But out of nowhere there was Lightening flying right above her head. Lightening then extended her wing as she gently pulled Zae out. But during this time there had been whirl wind sands building up and then to both Zae & Lightening's surprise the sand appeared in images of screens up in the air, stating "What do you think you are doing, this young lady will be taken from us for the mere part of her disturbing our sacred ground." Then Zae replied, "I meant no trouble" I have been lost and held captive in the grounds of Reyvanne. I was held against my will. But now I was just trying to find my way back to the Kingdom of Zamairria." Then the voices of the sand screen, "Whom is it that you know there?" Zae, answered, "It is a beautiful Goddess named Zuella." The sand screens, then replied. "Release here for she seeks out our Highness." Then gently Lightening started to pull Zae out safely. Zae said to them, "Thank you and who, what are you beings?" The voice said, "We are the protectors outside the wall of Kingdom of Zamairria, and no one gets through us if they do not serve our Goddess, whom stands for light energy, love and peace. So that you have mentioned our Goddess Zuella, we will allow you to go further." Zae stopped, and asked, "How is it that you guys exist?" The sand screens, then replied, "Many years ago, there was a kingdom called Wisterria, which ruled all outside of Zamairria. They were known to rule with no regards to any beings, as well as creatures. The ruled and lived through dark ways. They were barbaric in how they would kill people, there was a dark cloud over this kingdom. They were not empathetic to anyone but their own needs and wants. They had tried over the years, to be the only kingdom, to rule and have others join with their forces, and their beliefs. Which there is talk about sacrifices that they made from their own blood line. Goddess Zuella has always been of great light many of years ago, the Kingdom of Zamairria was below the ocean, was undersea. Which Goddess Zuella, possess the Light of the oceans and all that are within it, serve her for each being under the sea, belongs to the Goddess Light, Zuella. During this period, she had loved being of the sea, but one day many years ago. But with this all being done, many Kingdoms & Thrones, above water and under water were destroyed, and some renewed. Different realms of Kingdoms. Although Goddess Zuella, possessed many powers of under the sea, she transformed her energy to be able to be lighted in this world. But no one or anything truly knows the powers and gifts, that Goddess Zuella, has within her. All we hear, is that in finding true love, she will inherit gifts and lighted powers never held by anyone nor anything. But she must be able to give her heart fully to this being. Then she will become the illuminating force of no one can truly fathom. But that is was has been stated over hundreds of years."

Zae, then asked "Do you know much about where I just came from over at the coliseum, Kingdom of Reyvanne. I felt as if the man behind the mask was angry or had hatred in his heart. But as I ran off into the crowd of people there appeared to be spirits that were peaceful, such as the woman whom gave me the cloche to disguise myself, as I had asked her. There were multitudes of people that were there, but it was very strange, it almost appeared as if I can read people's spirits there. I felt many feelings of fear, but on other hand, lots of joy within their hearts and love. But many were fearful of things. There was a longing of peace within their hearts. Overall, they appeared to be quite confused as I. If I remember correctly, the man behind the mask called me Zae..." The voice of the sand screen, said, "What did this man call you, whom leads the throne of Kingdom of Reyvanne." "I believe the name he uttered was Zae. I started to recollect things, I do remember my mother, whom was his wife and Queen. But I remember him to be cruel at times. As he fought to be a nice person, but clearly there was such a dark feeling that I felt coming from him as he spoke." The sand screen said to me, "We believe you maybe the daughter that they tried to sacrifice and kill, but not quite sure. The name of that daughter was named Zae. The daughter was the only individual named with the letter Z. That was very odd, because all those of the kingdom of Reyvanne has names that all start with the letter R. But for your mother to name you, Zae. King Razeem, was ignited with rage, jealousy, and fury. But remained hidden so that the people would know nothing of the jealousy that drove him insane daily. There was talk that his wife, had an affair with someone of the kingdom of Zamairria, leaving King Razeem to question where or not Zae was his child. Unbearable, driving the king insane, drove him to conquest for the murder of his beloved wife, till one day the people found the Queens body to be ripped apart by five horses, tied to five poles, and her head, her legs, her hands ripped apart in five different directions, leaving her body there to disintegrate in the and vultures taking the remains." Zae, sobbing uncontrollably, not saying a word. "This is what was found of the remains of the body of Queen from our lighted beings. But no one knew exactly who did this horrific act. Because when Queen Resenti, was found nothing but bones, but there was talk about a ruby color garment gem necklace found on her neck." That seemed all to erie, for I wore a ruby color gem around my neck. "I believe you may be Zae," the sand screens voice uttered. By then, I realized that I was indeed, Zae daughter of Queen Resenti in the Kingdom of Reyvanne whom sat on the throne, until she had been murdered. Lightening, then murmured saying, "We must go, before they find you!" As I climbed up onto Lightening, wiping my tears, I turned around to the sand screeners and thank them for not harming me. Plus thanking them for allowing to know the story of my mother. As Lightening started to fly us up out of the sand area where I had fallen. Lightening notice a stampeded of chariots rushing over to where we were. So, we gallantly started to glide into the air, still fearing that at any time these chariots with soldiers had sparrow and arrow to shoot up at us. As we begun to elevate and trying to dodge arrows being shot up at us. I then heard a grunt coming from Lightening, but she was flying, and I had asked her "What's wrong?" With a tear falling from Lightening's eye, she said, "I will have no harm come to you as it did to your mother. Trust me and I will get you to safety." I then reached my right hand over to her side and began to pat her as we got higher and higher away from the chariots. We flew miles, and finally I notice on the ground's multitudes of palm trees and different type of trees so beautiful, plus a pond of water that I told Lightening that "I can't wait to drink, I am so thirsty." Lightening then descended as we got closer to the grounds, I can hear her panting harder and harder. I then asked, "What's wrong," she said, "No need to worry, but I will have to stay 5-6ft above the ground and see if you can jump off." I insisted on asking her, but she kept saying please just jump off. I then said, "ok will you drink water too!" As I jumped off onto the ground, I noticed a spear directly on the bottom of Lightening stomach. I then told Lightening "Please stay there in the air, I will help you." She said, "I will be ok!" I told her "This will hurt a lot, I will pull the spear from you, then you must fly down to the ground closer to the water. I could help you get water and try and patch you up with the leaves from the tree as well as the sand and make a pouch of mud to cover your wound." While I was seeking out remedies to patch up Lightening, she was able to drink while I attended her wounds. I was not sure of how anything would come about, but I tried anyway. Continuously, giving Lightening water by making a cup type holder from a leaf of the tree, I was able to give her drink while she lied there. I knew she was in excruciating pain simply because she panted hard as well as kept dozing off. I was fearful of losing her at this time for I had no idea whether anything I was doing would help. But I kept trying and making sure to check constantly if Lightening was still up. This went on for hours, but I put my head close to Lightening then I believed I passed out! I awoke by a wet like feeling on the side of my cheek. It was Lightening, she was up, I believe hours have passed by. Then I realized night was befalling and Lightening was in no condition to fly anywhere. So, I had to prepare us to sleep where we had landed. As I set a pouch of leaves to support Lightening's head, I gazed up into the sky where the stars lit up light making me, utterly making me feel at peace as I dozed off.

Chapter 9

The Child in the Tree

We awoke to sounds of horses galloping and stampeding our surroundings. I looked up and sat up to seeing stampedes of stallions and what appeared to be soldiers surrounding us. Lightening then got up and four horses gathered around her. The color of horses which approached Lightening, was yellow, red, orange and blue. These stallions had huddled together with Lightening, and in minutes all were sounded off to gather with each individual riding their stallions. Then in matter of minutes there were hundreds of stallions ascending into the sky with four of the stallions gathered around Lightening and I. Making sure that she was able to fly safely with me heading to where appeared to be the direction of where I believe the Kingdom of Zamairria was at. Then as I looked to the south where I recalled the dark clouds over the mountains, there seem to be a swarm of Black stampedes of animals flying in the sky towards are way. As they were heading our way, we seem to be flying faster as well as higher. The flying animals were hard to make as they were still distance from us. I then realize that these animals or flying objects were heading directly are way. Then Lightening said to the four stallions, "Let's go here, reroute and follow me." There were soldiers, guiding the stallions and we ended up turning back around heading the exact direction from where Lightening and I had left. That is where I had discovered the sand screens. There was so much commotion in the skies, as the black stampedes, were gaining closer, they appeared to be small dragons, with razor teeth. They were gnashing their teeth and you could hear clearly, because it sounded so loud. As we were flying in the skies, suddenly there was a crystal colored stallion that appeared to the right of me and Lightening, which had the individual name Zeheeles, which was Goddess Zuella's right hand person to the protector of the entire Zamairria. Zeheeles, then shouted in the sky to me, "You and Lightening must head back to Zamairria and we will lose the dragons so don't be afraid, Lightening will see to it that you get there safely." I am not knowing how to answer, but just quite in awe of what has taken place over the last few days. Hearing the voice of Lightening, stating, "We will head back to Zamairria," had comforted me in a mass way. We quickly turned away and headed back to where we were going earlier. We headed back towards Zamairria, and as we were flying in the sky, Lightening started towards the place where I had cared for her wounds. She stated," I need to rest a little before heading back and that she can use some water, we won't be long we will just stop off and rest up a bit and get enough water." I then told her, "No problem let's get some water, so you can feel better," for everything was all too sudden. She did not quite heal completely so that it was best for us to stop off for water. Get rested while we can for a bit, then we both agree to be on the same accord. As we got closer to the land, I can see the trees and noticed at the pond of water a small child drinking there. Lightening said to me, "Do you see the same thing I do?" She quickly flew faster to the area where the pond the child was drinking from, at the time that Lightening was descending the child looked up and notice us flying through. She then ran towards the trees, seeking shelter or trying to hide as if she were scared. But as we were landing on the ground, I had jumped off Lightening running towards the tree that the child seek refuge under. As I reached the tree where the child was at, I looked up and the child had climbed quickly up and stayed there hugging the tree making her way up to what appeared to be wood logs, built as if it were a place where you can live or hide. I gently call upon the child, "Could you kindly come down from there?" She said, "I don't know you, where are my friends of the trees, there is no one here!" I then asked, "What is your name?" The child does not reply. Still hugging the tree, I am not knowing what to do, so I strike up a conversation with the child and I told her that, "You are ok, don't worry nothing will hurt you. I know of you and your tree friends, because my good friend Goddess Zuella, told me about all of you." She then starts slowly down the tree, saying "Where are my tree friends?" I say, "I am not sure, but we can go look for them together." The child seems at ease and climbs down from the tree. She then hugged me tightly and said, "I am hungry. I want to find my friends." She then asked, "Is that a horse with wings?" I told her, "Yes! she is my friend and her name is Lightening. Would you care to meet her?" I said to the little girl, "What would you have me tell my friend, what your name is?" The child quickly replied, said "My name is Yzelle, and I am six years old." I said, "Wow! You are very brave and smart at that! Let's go meet my friend." We then started to walk towards the pond where

Lightening laid. Lightening then stood up and waited for me to speak, so I introduced the little girl, Yzelle to Lightening and to Yzelles surprise, Lightening spoke, saying "Hello my friend, how are you?" Yzelle , said, "Wow! You talk and you fly?" I said, "Of course!" She said, "I am so happy, I have always dreamt of a flying horse, but never did I think they would talk." We all then sat around the pond for a few minutes and then I said to "Yzelle, you will go with us to the Kingdom of Zamairria, where Goddess Zuella waits for Lightening." Yzelle, was exceptionally excited and could not wait for us to take off. We then prepared for our departure, excited knowing that we are about to fly on a horse. Suddenly as we started to ascend, Lightening and I noticed in the air a black object flying towards our way. Not wanting Yzelle, to get hysterical, Lightening and I both kept our cool, still trying to make out what was it that was flying our way. But incidentally, the little girl looked up seen what we were trying to make out in the air. I then said to Lightening, "It seems to be one of the creatures that were chasing us earlier, but there appears to be only one. It is a dragon; it's shooting fire out towards us!" Lightening then said, to Yzelle and I, "Hold on tight, I will be flying quite fast." We both latched onto Lightening's reins and held on tightly. Lightening then started to fly dodging the fire balls being shot at us. Remarkably no balls of fire, hit us, Lightening's, flying skills were impeccable. I was very impressed although we tried to lose the little dragon it seemed to gain footage on us. So then suddenly Lightening said, "We must land somewhere to lose this dragon!" I told her, "Do what you think must be done to protect us." So then as I looked down, we were in a place which appeared to be quite dark shadow by over casted clouds. There was a huge fortress that was fully darkened, black trees, rugged terrain. It seems to be a castle of some sort. There were many of black crows flying about and surrounding the ground. This building seems to be of old castle looking with round towers with a long bridge made of wood, roughly 30ft long from the castle to the grounds. It seems to have guards with arrows and swords guarding its towers. This whole place had such an eerie vibe to it! There were guards surrounding the tower on top. We then heard horns sounding off and it seem to be that the guards and people were being alerted to our entrance of the grounds. Plus, the dragon was right behind us. Suddenly we heard a huge squawking sound in the air. It was the dragon being shot by the guards who guarded this castle. Sighed with relief thinking that we are totally out of danger, we landed on the grounds and were greeted with guards that were outside the compound of the castle. So, as we looked towards them, they ran towards us, bum rushed us and grabbed Yzelle, and me, and took Lightening by her reins. Taking us inside to what appeared to be their castle which was old rugged. There were multitudes of people surrounding us, as if they were part of this culture of the people of the castles. They then took us inside of the compound and there was a hall like way that seemed to be lit with little torches that hung through the halls. As we walked through there were doors set right in front as they drug us through the compound. It seems to be as if there was darkness surrounding the whole vicinity. While being drug through the halls, I noticed on the doors, a picture of skulls above the handles with a huge torch which lit the door brightly.

The guards then took one of the handles and turned the knob, for the door to open, and as it did, inside looked dark with a single chair, where sat this man, in a dark grey and black cloche. Covering his entire body. He also, had a steel mask screen, over his face plus a crown made of twine black wooden crown worn above his head. On the top of the tip of crown, there was a carving of a skull in white. This man said, "Whom are these two people you guard brought into my throne. This is the Kingdom of "Wazerria", no one is welcome to the Kingdom of my throne, unless I have invited them. Who are these young ladies that you bring in front of me here! I have ordered all of my Kingdom to make sure that no outsiders enter into our Kingdom unless ordered by me, King Waes, ruler to this Throne! Take these two out of my site and do away with them." Immediately the young girl, Yzelle, started screaming as we were grabbed and drugged out of there.

Chapter 10

Trapped in Wazerria

Now Back in the Kingdom of Zamairria, there are sounds of horns being sounded off, for the people to prepare for a search. Goddess Zuella, has notified her right hands at the palace to send out re-enforcements for backing in search for the young lady, "Zae" as well as her personal guide, white stallion, name "Lightening". Now everyone who the Goddess entrust are being disbursed outward for somewhat called a search party. This is being done immediately. Suddenly Goddess Zuella, and states, "I will join in this search for these two", not knowing that the young girl from the tree children has now joined, Zae and Lightening. As they prepare chariots, suddenly stampedes of the flying stallion, probably four dozens of them returned into the palace, stating to the Goddess, "You might want to ride with us your highness, because where the young lady and Lightening have gone, you will need us to get you there," Goddess Zuella asked to the other flying stallions, "Where is it that you think they may have gone." The stallion answered, "It appears that they had gone into the Kingdom of Waes." Goddess quickly replied, "We must be off before it is too late! I am feeling that there is such a surge of urgency needed on behalf of Lightening and the lady we had in our care." The flying stallion then stated are you sure about this, that you are wanting to go on this search." Zuella, said, "I am sure, and we must go at once." Then off they all went, while in the air, Goddess Zuella then makes a certain sound as if she is singing, and you see sand storms arising as if they were headed that way, but as they got closer the stampede of four dozen with Goddess Zuella, suddenly the sand storms subsided in the air and they joined us swaying in back of them as if they were following the Goddess. Suddenly, one of the stallions next to the Goddess, said "Look at the mass amount of water heading over the mountains, it appears to be a major flooding of some type." With great surprise, there were major creatures in the air and on ground rapidly catching up to us and as they did, Goddess Zuella, started to sing the most beautiful sound and nodding her head smiling as if she were greeting the water, the sand storm and all the creatures flying in back of them. It was remarkable, it seemed as if the Goddess had control over all that had joined them. Then Goddess Zuella, spoke in the air, and her voice carried throughout the skies and the seas seem to have acknowledged her presence. She kept singing throughout the flight in the air, there was a huge amount of lighted energy that progressed throughout! So, in the gathering of all that joined Goddess Zuella, it was blatantly obvious that these creatures and the water, sand and air were controlled by Zuella herself. Amazing how the water just flowed across the lands, flowing in all paths, but moving to where there were no destructions done. It was like n ever seen before. The sandstorms just gallantly winding in certain place without destruction to anything! What a site to be seen, never ever on the face of the planet could this occur! Seemingly, the capabilities of what the

Goddess has, was quite breathtaking, completely in awe of what her powers were imbedded in her. Obliviously, Goddess Zuella controlled the energy of Light, amongst various elements and creatures. This is a sight to be seen, for this will never take place again. The flight was somewhat lengthy, but amazingly done. As they approached closer to the Kingdom of Wazerria, they were able to spot the dark overshadowing cloud above Wazerria. As they were flying suddenly torches of fire arrows were being shot at them! With cannon balls of fire as well, being shot at the Goddess and her fleet of people and flying stallions. As the fire arrows and cannon fire were being shot up, they were immediately put out when the seas that were following Goddess Zuella, shot tunnels of water to defeat and put out fire immediately. There was no harm to Goddess, simply because all the fleet she brought with her, had clearly protected her and her stampede of stallions as well as her right-hand guides that flew with her on the journey to seek out Lightening and the young lady, "Zae". She then made a statement to all her followers, "Stand guard in the air, I will go down with a dozen of stallions and my right-hand people to see about the whereabouts of Lightening and the young lady. All will adhere to my command, none of you are to do anything and wait for my return. If for some reason I do not return, you are fully to do what it is to be done in seeking justice with Light and overtake this Kingdom that lives in complete darkness. You all are fully equipped to put this Kingdom of Wazerria, back in perspective and allow nothing but lighted energy to reside there. So, I will go down now and wait for my call." One of the individuals who is her right hand stated to Zuella, "Your highness please stay behind and allow us to go on your behalf." Zuella then said, "Ok go on and I will stay behind, notify me on what is happening right away, or tap into your mind calling me and letting me know, I will clearly hear your call. Then it is done, we will hold off in the skies, awaiting your journey down. General "Zerak" I will bless your journey so be blessed on your task and I will await your response! If you come across trouble, immediately notify me." General, Zerak, states to his ruler, "Goddess Zuella, we are off now. I will call upon you if needed." As they started to fly away and descend gradually, there were arrows and spears shot up to Zerak and his two dozen guards with their stallion, and without Zuella. Zerak and his fleet landed safely and the soldiers of King Waes were there standing guard awaiting their arrival. But during their arrival, the leader of King Waes, right hand named, "Wesielk" was ready and ask Goddess Zuella people "What is the purpose of you emposing into our kingdom with no authority or granted access to our Kingdom. Zerak answered "We are on journey to find the young lady that was in our care as well as the right-hand flying stallion, which belongs to Zuella, the Goddess of the Light of Kingdom Zamarria." "There are two young ladies that entered our kingdom without our Kings permission therefore they will be put to death. You all will join them for coming to our sacred ground with no entrance of access granted for you all." Wesielk then replied to his guards, "Seize all of them." Zerak rapidly stated "We come in peace to retrieve what does not belong to you people." Suddenly two guards from Wazerria, speared two of the tribe of Zamarria as well as their stallions, out of nowhere. Killing them instantly. To Zeraks, surprise he was taken and blind folded with everyone else, being beaten as well as drug, and tied up! Within minutes Zerak and his fleet found themselves put in a dungeon, which they can hear they roar of tigers. But suddenly they also heard female voices stating "Are they ok!" Zerak, said "Are you bounded," Zae then answered "No!" Zeraks, says "Are you the lady from the Kingdom of Zamairria that we were caring for at the palace." Zae then said "Yes, but I found the little girl and her name is Yzelle, plus we have no idea where Lightening might be." Zerak then quickly said, "Can you help untie me and take off these blinders." Zae, got up then went to help! Zerak, said "You must move quickly before they come back to kill us." As I help take off his blinders, suddenly a great roar from the next cage uttered. Zerak said "Hurry, please." I then freed his hands, then he helped the rest of them, and to all our surprise the tiger was right at the cage entrance as if was ready to devour something or someone. Still moving swiftly, the General was able to get his people free, plus talk to the little girl named Yzelle to help put her to ease. During the shuffling, Zerak, found a way out that would mean having to go through the cage where the tigers were. That would be suicide, but then guards from Wazerria approached and noticed everyone unbounded and quickly open the door to get things in control. But then Zerak and his people fought back overpowering the guards and taking control. Zerak, quickly had his people guide us out and took us out the castle of Wezerria, leaving us at the tunnel, while they went and seek out all the stallions that were being held captive. They found the place where the stallions were being held captive then freed them, but to their surprise it was all in lieu of being caught again. Gallantly Zerak and his soldiers were confronted by Kings Waes men and they started to fight, slicing one another, killing each other, this gone on for quite some time! But some of the men of Goddess Zuella were able to get stallions and bring them our way so that we can get away! But in doing so some of the men were killed trying to help us get away! One of the soldiers from Kingdom of Zamairria had approached me and Yzelle with stallions telling us get on and the stallions will fly us to safety. We were reluctant to leave them, because of the chaotic drama fighting that was going on. The guard insisted to get on and leave now. So, me and Yzelle, immediately got on stallions.

Chapter 11

Falling Kiss

The stallions made sure to secure me and Yzelle, then ascended during our ascension, we were secured but as our flight took off, we were being shot at with multiple fire balls, spears, and arrows. I felt an impact and suddenly felt a sensation of pain in my right leg! As I looked down, I was hit with an arrow piercing, I looked down and the arrow was inside my leg! Suddenly, I felt lightheaded and excruciating pain ran up my leg. As we were ascending, I suddenly felt as if I were going to pass out! I started to lose my sighting and believed I passed out falling off the stallion into the air, but to my biggest surprise was caught by another stallion, to whom had Goddess Zuella on them. Goddess Zuella, caught me as I fell from the stallion into the sky! She then grabbed me to secure me on her stallion. I looked up and to my surprise I gazed into the eyes of Goddess Zuella, who had taken off her sash across her mouth. I felt her stare as if she were wanting me somehow, so I just went with my gut as much pain as I was in, I reached closer to Goddess Zuella, and then kissed her, she then kissed me back, there was so much passion in our kiss that I forgot my pain for a few minutes. I then held on tight and found that Zuella had designated the stallion to take us somewhere away from where we were at! I had wanted to be there locking lips with Zuella, I found myself to mesmerized just falling out of the sky literally straight into the hands of the Lady Goddess. Talk about a dream come true. How fascinating on the feeling of emotions that were flowing inside of me although I felt pain to my leg. It really did not seem to have an impact for at this very minute I was in a bliss. Just found me in complete utterly hypnotized by her kiss. I felt a bit lightheaded and seemed to keep dozing off while Goddess Zuella and the stallion were getting me to safety. Apparently, I had dozed off, and suddenly as I woke, I found myself in a most beautifully elegant scenery of waterfalls, and lovely white rocks with beautiful trees surrounding with the sunlight beaming through streaks of ray of light hitting myself. I found myself, awoken by the gentle soft hand wetting my forehead with water spilt on my forehead. Then I started to get up and noticed the beauty surrounding! It appears we were in a crystal-like scenery. The place was magical, plus the colors were very vibrant! There were lady bugs, exquisite looking birds and butterflies of every color possible that you can think of! I looked up and started getting up for I my head was on her lap, Goddess Zuella just sat right beside me stroking my face as she watered the top of my head! As I was sitting up, I noticed that there was no pain in my leg, and the arrow was no longer in my leg! I went to pull up my pants at the leg to see about my wound, but there was no wound to be found. I then looked at Goddess Zuella and seen that she had a slight smile. I then asked her, "Did you do anything to me, because my wound is gone." She did not reply, so we then talked about what had happened, I then quickly remembered "Where is Yzelle?" Goddess Zuella, said "Who's Yzelle?" I then told Zuella, "She is the little girl that Lightening, and I had found in the desert along the trees." Goddess Zuella, said immediately, "The little girl you both found may have been the child that the tree children came to us and needed help to find. That it is amazing, but where is she?" I then replied, "She was with me, on the flying stallion taking us to safety and all I remembered was I was passing out and had fell off the horse into the sky. Then you caught me, Zuella!" The Goddess then replied, "If she was with you on one of my stallions, then the child would be okay! But do you recall of where you come from or even know your name?" I then answered her, and stated, "Other people have called me Zae! When they had told me my name, I started to recollect, memories of the past which were quite unpleasant!" I began telling Goddess Zuella, all the memories that I started to remember. Zuella, just sat there and listened while I started to recollect memories. She seemed to be very attentive to my story of memories. It was such a peaceful feeling knowing that I was able to share what I started to remember with the Goddess. She was such a delight to confide in. Then as I was feeling a sign of relief and speaking, surge of fire balls appeared to be shooting at us burning what was around us! We quickly looked up to see a fleet of black dragons flying towards us. They were deep black colored with fiery red and yellowish eyes. They kept shooting fire towards us, and we quickly ran towards the back of the waterfall where there appeared to be a cave lit with light crystalized blue. As we ran in the dragons seem to not be able to come through for Goddess Zuella, had did something mystical, as putting a barrier wall between the waterfall and the dragons. I then grabbed Zuella's hand and told her

"Follow me" We will go through the cave that has been lit with crowns that had beautifully lit torches to guide our way. As we started to walk through, the scenery was quite intriguing, the walls were of crystals and gems, but of blues, deeper and brighter lights that seem to shining the crystals to have them glow as if it were lighting up, just massive illumination of light being lit up! But the cave ran deep, and it seem to be cut off into sections. The first section we had approached had colorful water running against the wall. The feeling was quite beautiful, I was wondering in my head, why is it that Goddess Zuella, did not seemed to be nervous or scared at all. Holding her hand, was still so soft and no sign of fear. But as we started to go through the first section, we had come across a carved sculpture of an image of a woman wearing a beautiful designed crown, with emeralds imbedded in the wall, plus to lightening bolts on each side of her face. But I suddenly had a sharp pain go to my head, and then an image of the face on the crown, it was an image of my mother! 'What?" Goddess Zuella, asked me, if I was alright, but I could not make out what was going on in my head. I kept it to myself about the crown carving of the lady's picture. But for some apparent reason, Goddess Zuella, said "This crown seems to be of my Kingdom in Zamairria. I am unfamiliar with this crown, and I will find out who this lady's carved image is." I then got more flashes of this lady, and it was my mother. Then I finally said to Goddess Zuella, "That is a carving of my mother's image on the crown." Goddess Zuella implied that, "The two lightning bolts on any crown from my kingdom, Is sign of being directly lineage of those who have governed the Kingdom of Zamairria and to have been know of the family of Royalty before I came to surface from the ocean." Goddess Zuella, then replies, "I should be bowing to you for your lineage is what made Kingdom of Zamairria through all these centuries."

Chapter 12

Retreat

Over by the Kingdom of Wizerria, there was battling of their people and the people of Zamairria. There was war in the skies as well as on ground, but many were getting injured. Although they were still fighting in the air, Goddess Zuella and Zae were nowhere to be found. But meanwhile, the stallions and troops of people from the Kingdom of Zamairria were getting injured and killed. There were multiple dragons being disbursed with fire shooting out of their mouths. Then came this huge snake looking dragon, ten times the size of what the other dragons were sized up to be. This dragon, had the King of Waes riding on its back, shouting to Kingdom of Wizerria, "We will conquer and destroy all that comes with this Kingdom of Zamairria, to disturb my grounds." While proclaiming his authority in the air, suddenly a bright sky-blue stallion appeared with General Zerak, from the Kingdom of Zamairria, he answered, "You call yourself King Waes, you will not cause more destruction to what you have already with your Kingdom." The battles continue in the air shooting of fire balls as wells as swords that were electrifying as they clashed with one another. Suddenly the skies roared with thunder and lightning, allowing the fleet from Zamairria to have to retreat seeking out where there injured people had fallen.

While scattered throughout, the people of Zamairria, seemed to be falling in multitudes along with their stallions. Others grabbing them and trying to retreat to safer grounds. To try and save others, they were told to retreat to sand screen grounds. They quickly disbursed and as they did, General Zerak had gotten hit with a fire ball on shoulder, then the dragon snake which King Wae had ridden, had shot out some type of venom spray landing on General Zerak's face, blinding him instantly. The stallion in charge of riding General Zerak, had told him "Wrap his hands around tightly, so that you won't fall off while I get you to safety quickly." The General then replied, "Fly as fast as you can away from here, because I cannot see anything." The stallion then replied, "Yes sir!" and was off speedily trying to get to safety. There was a great shout in the sky as you heard the thunders roaring and lightning striking. The great shout was the voice of King Waes, commanding all of his fleet and dragons to return to their campgrounds. So then crowd of battling in the air as well as the grounds had disbursed immediately! Back at the sand screen campground. Was where the people of Zamairria had gathered to attend to their wounded. Somehow, General Zerak, made his way there to be attended too quickly. The sand screen people ended up putting up a barrier wall to protect them while trying to get to their wounded and the others whom they had lost along the way. General Zerak, then stated, to one of his commanders to "Get a party of seven of the best fighters and prepare an elite search for the Goddess Zuella, for we are not knowing of her whereabouts. This search team must prepare and go at once quickly, for the Goddess may need support immediately." The commander then replied, "We will prepare our people to go on mission for the Goddess Zuella, seek out our Ruler so that we can secure our fleet and get back to our Kingdom of Zamairria for the children of the tree await us." Suddenly a soldier came to where the General Zerak, was camped out at. The soldier walked up holding a little girl's hand walking alongside each other. The General said, to the soldier "Who is this young child?" The soldier then replied and said "This child stated that she was with another lady, but the lady got shot and had fallen off their stallion. But that's all the child knows." So, then the General, put it together and stated, "She must have been the young lady which we originally had in our care. I know that we must hurry and send out the search party for the Goddess as well as the young lady who had fallen. Seek out them immediately. Prepare and then shortly be on the way for the search! Make sure the child is well taken care of, here in the sand screens compound there are rash ins that the sand screen peoples have stored away for issues like these that arise. Confirm that the young child is secure, and I will make sure that our people watch over her here at the camps. Prepare and leave immediately. We will await and hold off behind while you and your group go and see whether you guys are able to fine the Goddess. We will stand by for a day and if your search is not back yet then we will come for you all! So, take your team and execute what I have commanded from you!" Then suddenly the commander left and prepared his team for departure. The General, was being cared for as others attended to his wounds as well as his eyes, for somewhat reason the venom that the dragon had shot into his face made him blind instantly. They called in a couple of the Lighted beings which had joined them and ask for them to have healings done for the General's eyes. But no of them can seem to get his vision back with clarity. The General stated, "Im still unable to see clearly." So, the Lighted Beings tried all they knew but still could not bring the General's vision back to be clear. So, the General was asked to rest up as the search party, was on their way in search of the Goddess of Zamairria. The search party only had seven of their best fighters, warriors and seven black stallions. They all were fully equipped with gear of weapons of swords, spears, belts with shooting crystal balls and lightning bolt looking dagger arrows. They then had taken off in search of Zuella & the lady (Zae), whom they cared for over in the Kingdom of Zamairria. It begun to get dark, and they started to burn camp preparing for the evening to hit. Tents were put up and torches were lit to keep light around the camp. The child then ran up to the General, asking for the lady who had help her, "Where did she fall too? Did she die?" The child was crying while the General asked one of his people to bring the child close for him to speak too! The General then asked, "Why are you crying little one?" The child said, "The young lady, was very protective of me and extremely kind and made me feel safe." The General then replied, "No need to worry little one, everything will turn out well, ok!"

Chapter 13

Cave of Memories

Surprised of her family lineage, Zae began to remember who her mother was! She remembered stories of when her mother would tell her as a child. Where she came from and how she ended up in the Kingdom Reyvanne. Zae, concluded and said to Goddess Zuella, "I believe I am regaining my memory. Mainly about my mother and what she would tell me as a child over in the Kingdom of Reyvanne." Goddess Zuella, said to Zae, "I believe I know of her story. Before I came into the Kingdom of Zamairria, I was of another world which was under the sea. That world was called, Ozerria! When the world here had been reversed of turning upside down, I had no choice but to come above and recover the lighted structure that once ruled Kingdom of Zamairria. I was guided up higher light energy to be brought from the surface so that I may rule. But as I was being brought up to do so, I was enlightened by many of stories of the one who once ruled this Kingdom, which her name then was Zeirriah. The story was that she had fallen in love with an outsider and chose to leave her Kingdom to please the King of Reyvanne, whom she had fallen in love with after losing her love here at Kingdom of Zamairria. There was mentioned soon after losing her love here at Zamairria, she married the King of Reyvanne and soon was pregnant. The King always, believed that the Child she bore was not truly his. But he could not prove it till this day! There were stories of the King of Reyvanne being full of rage, feeling as if his Queen may have had an affair and bore someone else's child. But that remains to be seen for no one knows what became of the Queen of Reyvanne." Then Zae replied, "I believe that the story you speak of, is my mother! Her life was taken drastically from me. I do remember things about how cruel that man was towards my mother and me. This man is so cruel, that his world was full of misery. He always claimed my mother was betraying him and that she had been seeing someone else. But right now, we must keep moving and try and see if there is any way out of the cave so that we can join the others, plus I must see if Yzelle is ok!" Goddess then said, "There is nothing to worry about the little girl, I am sure that she is in great hands. If she were with you on one of the stallions, then I am sure my people have her and are looking over her." As we progressed into the cave, we had come across an area where there was a whirlpool of water that was quite illuminating with different types of sea creatures in it, and it appear to be deep to a point where it may connect the ocean of water under. But did not quite know for sure, for we did not take a dive into the water. This section of the cave was lit up with greenish color neon lights with a touch of sky-blue streaks but had such a beautiful glow with the breaking of the current. As we turned around to see our surroundings, it appears to be lit with the same type of crowns that were in the first part of the cave. Suddenly a somewhat looking seahorse about 5ft. brought its head out of the ocean whirlpool, and quickly Goddess Zuella sang a mystical melody, and it seemed as if the seahorse looking creature totally understood and acknowledge her. It was very appealing for the eye to see. So then still in awe, I discovered another path that led us into the cave of sand that had such beautiful fine bristles of multiple colors in the grain. But oddly, there was the crown face with the two lightning bolts and image of my mother's face, being revealed as the sand on the ground brushed back. I then hesitated and said to Goddess Zuella, "Are you familiar with these caves?" She said "I will soon tell you the meaning of these caves. I do recall the legend of your mother now. When we are secured in Zamairria, I will be more than happy to share with you what I have been told about the caves of the (Lighted Waterfalls)." I try to impose another question to Zuella but could not resist to kiss her again! So, I then reached over and kissed her saying to her, "I feel this immense emotion towards you but cannot make out what this means." Zuella, then smiled like usual, and said "We must be on our way, let's try and seek out a way to get to the others, for I know there must be a search party being disbursed to look for us." I then told Zuella, "We must talk!", she answered, "We will, after we get to Zamairria." I then agreed to seek out an exit, but as we started to walk more into the cave, we came to an opening which had beautifully shaped vines, made with colorful leaves. Directly in front of us lied a huge white rose which open as we entered it! This rose measured 10x10 having a beautifully hand-woven carpet(5x7) and as the beautiful rose started to open back it's stemmed the carpet raised and I was in shock! No way! This is truly a dream! Could this be a flying carpet? As the carpet elevated, I was told by Zuella, "get on!" I looked at her and said, "You're kidding right." I said, "In the Kingdom of Zamairria, does everything fly?" She said, "Mostly everything that I had wished for at one time." So, I proceeded to get on, along with Goddess Zuella, and boy this carpet held us. Then suddenly the vines pulled back away, making an opening door so that we were able to see the outside of the cave. We had found our way out! Goddess Zuella, said "Just sit back and we will be on our way." I said, "Are you sure?" Zuella, then comforted me and said, "Just be at ease the carpet will take us to where we must go!" The carpet then proceeded to fly with us on it and the vines shuttled the door close as if there was no opening. The day was lit beautifully, and the carpet ride was so breathtaking. I found it to be equally as exciting and exhilarating as riding with Lightening the flying stallion. But like Zuella mentioned for me to be at ease, I totally did so, and took in the carpet ride. As we progressed in the sky taking in the beauty of all scenery, we talked and spoke of the journey that I have taken since the people of Zamairria first found me. Zuella asked, "Did you have any other sisters or brothers?" I said, "Yes, I believe I have one brother, whom is the King of Reyvanne's true heir." Zuella, said "Is he your father Zae?" I then said, "There has been stories that I heard, but my mother never mentioned anything to me. I feel as if I am not this King's daughter, for he is very cruel, and very similar to the King of Wezerria, where your people had rescued me and Yzelle. There was good and bad over in the Kingdom of Reyvanne. People were afraid to stand up for goodness."

Chapter 14

Zuella and Her Light

While waiting on the return of the search party, General Zerak, was panting back and forth wondering what the outcome of the search party that was disbursed to seek out the Goddess Zuella, and the young lady whom had fallen from the stallion in the sky. As the the General asked of information on the update. Suddenly the sand screens started to brush through the air and whirlwind of sand started to gather up making sandstorms within the air. But not actually knowing what is happening suddenly all people and stallions were back during chaos being under attack. But the sand screens were doing their job in being the protected wall of holding off the dragons, plus other creatures in the air, looking like huge beast of vultures, herds and herds of them. The campground where the people of Zamairria were camping has been attacked, by the creatures and dragons of Wazerria. Everyone has been in an uproar, because of the shooting with fireballs from the dragons flying above their camp. General Zerak, is trying to control the people but not being able to see anything clearly had made him, frustrated! But he remains cool, and was calling out to any of his troops, to find the little girl, Yzelle. Frantically panicking, the General then shouted someone find the girl. Suddenly, while being under attack, there was a soldier by the name of Zeem, answered and stated, "I found the young girl." Immediately the General was relieved but still in commanding mode, to be able to control the atmosphere and the people of Zamairria. But the attack was getting heavier, as the enemy started to move in closer to the camp, burning multitudes of camps. One of the soldiers ran towards the General and said, that "There are soldiers from Wazerria, riding on the backs of dragons and the vultures!" Then the General shouted to everyone "Be on guard and make sure that the enemy does not take over, fight with all you have and don't give up. We must fight back. So do not retreat." As the war was getting rough throughout, the battle was starting to get worst as the soldiers and enemies started to land. Suddenly, the enemy seemed to close in and jumped off of their dragons and vultures, and started to slay any of the people of Zamairria, the battle went on as both sides were falling, the sand screens were just on standby as well as the ocean water stood still on the grounds not making any types of moves. Still around the people of Zamairria, the water and sand screens seemed as if they were waiting on direction. But would not move into where the battle of Zamairria and Wazerria were fighting against each other. Seemingly it was rather gruesome, the death toll on the side of Zamairria started to grow. So now, the people were starting to feel a bit hopeless. As their hopes were failing them, suddenly they heard a loud but mystical sound coming above the sky. Suddenly the sand screens formatted the whirlwind and the ocean water started to wash through the land taking only the enemy and the sand screens. It appeared to be Goddess Zuella, and Zae flying on a carpet with the Goddess standing above with her hands extended as if she were speaking to the ocean and sand to obey her command. Zuella, then sang a song where the ocean then formed up into a somewhat looking tornado whirlpool looking feature and began to swallow up the enemy, but while this was happening the other half of the enemy of Wazerria, flead and over half had retreated back and seemed to have disappeared. As the ordeal of the battle subsided, it was blatantly obvious that Goddess Zuella, showed up just in the nick of time. It was such an illuminating fascinating scene to see Zuella, in her lighted realm, controlling what no man had control over. It was spectacular! I was quite amazed on the whole ordeal of this taking place. This was surreal, quite unimaginable! But I bore witness to the event of what Goddess Zuella had done, with the sand screens, and water whirlpool in the air that traveled on the grounds and moved to capture the enemy! Our flight on the carpet, started to descend and within minutes we touched ground. As we landed, we had looked over and seen General Zerak, was guided towards our way. He greeted me and Zuella and brought the Goddess up to speed with what had occurred. The Goddess then asked the General, "Why are your eyes covered with cloth and why is it that you have someone holding your arm as if you were guided to me!" The Genereal then replied, "I had been shot with venom of the dragon snake and it left my vision blurred." Immediately Goddess Zuella, lifted her hands towards the General and moved his cloth, there seem to be a beam of light coming from the Goddess's hand towards the General, within minutes the General was able to see clearly. We were all amazed on what just happened to the General, which Goddess Zuella cured his blurred vision. The General immediately stated, "Your highness I must prepare our people for battle!" Zuella stated, "Let us gather our people and see the count of lives lost!" General said, there is no time, they will try and attack again. Nevertheless, the elite force whom the General sent prior to the arrival of Zuella, had also returned. Zuella, had stated to everyone, "Seize and reconstruct for they all need to rest their bodies and heal up!" She will command the ocean as well as the sand screens to place a safety wall around the campground for the time being. "Surely, the people must regain their strength and faith as we prepare for any future attacks. We must see that the enemies do not reach the Kingdom of Zamairria for the tree children have stayed behind with my counsel and people to look over the children and protect them." The General stated, "The enemy has creatures that can-do damage to our Kingdom if we do not go there." Zuella, said "keep the battle here on the grounds of the Sand Screen!" Immediately Zae replied, and said, "Is this not the area, close to the coliseum where I was held captive as well?" General Zerak, stated, "The Kingdom of Reyvanne is not but a way from here. If we were to estimate days, the trip to the Kingdom of Reyvanne is a four-day travel by foot!" Zae then said, "It is not a place that I would ever think of revisiting ever again!" Zuella, said "The people must secure their areas, and attend to the wounded, plus make sure that we all here regain our strength. We must unite in a bit so that I may address the people of Zamairria, to reassure them that we will be okay!" Night began to fall slowly, while the people were getting their areas in order. Trying to set camp, for being able to get rest and be on standby for anything! They had naturalized the campground and then came to where Goddess Zuella stood, and Zuella then approached and spoke to her people giving them light and love energy, plus built their self within to prepare them for whatever awaits their future. The people then disbursed after the talk with Goddess Zuella and went to get rest. Zae, then approached Zuella to finish their conversation and then Zuella, said "We shall finish our conversation soon!", looking at Zae as if there were unspoken words and feelings that needed to be addressed! The night befell and the campground seemed to fall to silence while the people of Zamairria, had gone to bed. Goddess Zuella, and Zae then met by the campfire that seem to be burning lowly with sparks of ash from fire coming out of the camp. So, we then started to converse, while staring into each other's eyes, plus Goddess had taken her sash off to where I was able to see her face clearly. I was inclined to the conversation taking place at the time. I was so mesmerized by Zuella's illuminating beauty. We then started to discuss the story of the "Lighted Waterfall". She has known for over decades the true story, about Zae's mother but had no idea that the story was true! Zuella, has always believed that the story had been mythical. Soon enough, the story that Zuella knew of, was quite extraordinary. She began to tell me the story that she had heard about her mother, who was known to be a legend in the eyes of the Kingdom of Zamairria. It seems all so peaceful throughout the campground; everyone seems to have been getting rest, others were attending the wounded while helping them to get better rested. During the night as we continued to talk to each other, the night was beautifully lit, with multitudes of stars as bright illuminating the night as the spark of fire from camp seek to catch the igniting beauty of Zuella.

Chapter 15

Goddess Zerriah

While sitting with Zuella, Zae had asked her to
kindly share the story of her mother, that she has been
told about! Zuella, then started to get into the story, and
she said to Zae. "There was talk of long ago, before I had
come from the sea, there was a legendary Goddess
named, Zerriah whom I believe this day is to be your
mother. She was the mother of all, and had ruled over the
Kingdom of Zamairria, once known as Light of Paradise!
She had ruled by far all that is and fell in love with one
of the servants. Lots of the people frowned upon their
relationship, simply because she was by far superior to
all and she ended up falling in love with a man who is
not within her caliber. She ruled the galaxies in the skies
and had the one and only, God almighty to report too!
She was the most powerful ever to rule, she had control
over the seas, galaxies, creatures on ground in air, as well
as other planets. The man whom she had fallen in love
with was named, Zuleen. He was brought to the
Kingdom, Light of Paradise, simply to work for the true
Goddess, but somewhere down the road they both ended
up falling in love. Goddess Zerriah, was fighting to be
with Zuleen, but the Goddess's did not agree. When she
was impregnated, she then was casted out of the Light of
Paradise, and the story was told that Zuleen, was taken

to where no one would ever find him, nor will they ever see each other again. The Goddess Zerriah did not agree with the Goddess's decision; therefore, she was not hurt by stripped away of all her powers, and casted out the sands the desert. No one was to help her because she chose to have the baby from the servant and not rule the Kingdom, Light of Paradise. The tale is that she wondered about in the desert sand, and fondly was taken by the people of Reyvanne, where she became the wife, Queen of King Rezeem, which ultimately led to her death, according to how the tale has been told. So, I am so sorry about your mother, Zae!" Zae cried softly and tears had fallen down her face, as Zuella then reached over to pull her face up, Zae began to cry extensively. As Zuella, reached over and pulled Zae closer to try and console her. The campfire started to get more dim, and suddenly Zae put her head on Zuella's lap and just cried herself to sleep. While the night befell, all the campground had appeared to be silent that you could hear a pin drop.

Chapter 16

The Sudden Attack

As the light from the sunlight start to brighten up the campground as morning hit, the people of Zamairria were awaken by the stampede of chariots awaiting and shooting at the wall of protection that Zuella had placed over the camp. Suddenly the entire people of Zamairria awoke and prepared for battle for it appeared to be soldiers from the Kingdom of Reyvanne, who had showed up to attack the campgrounds! Goddess Zuella, then addressed her people and stated, "You will battle and defend each other," but reluctantly was sure that she would be able to protect her people. Zae suddenly stood up and said to Zuella, "Before anything takes place, before we go to war, I must be truthful with you." Zuella, then said "What is it?" As they were both in the middle of speaking, Zae just shouted, "I believe I am in love with you!" Zuella, said "We must discuss this later." Zae then replied, "There may not be a later." Zuella, briefly said, "I must not fall in love, for I do have a Kingdom to rule, plus once I have fallen some of my powers will be stripped away." Zae continued to shout, "I love you!" at least 3-4 times, please say something to me!" Zae shouted. Zuella, says "They will know, my feelings and I will lose control of my ruling powers." Zea shouted "At least tell me whether you feel anything for me or not!"

Zuella, had given a look of despair and immense love, but could not utter the words, in fear of losing the power to protect her people. "Once the Goddess's, know my feelings and emotions towards you, truly my powers will be taken." Zae, states "That's absurd! I do not believe that the Goddess's have the right to take away your power's, just for displaying that you love me! If you do, that is!" Zuella, then turns to her General Zerak, who suddenly appears and shouts to him "You must prepare the people of Zamairria for battle and they must not retreat." Zae, then turned around and started to walk away from Zuella, turning her head slightly to glance once more upon Zuella, Zuella stated to Zea "I love you too!" Then spear entered Zae's chest, immediately taking her to the ground, and to Zuella's surprise the protected walls where no longer up and the people of Zamairria were under attack! Zuella, then made a scream that no one has ever heard, and fell to her knees. Zuella, was deeply in surprise of what just happened. Zae, is lying on the ground with the spear launched in her chest! General Zerak, then grabs the Goddess and tries to get her to safety, leaving Zae on the ground. The Goddess screaming for her soldiers to help Zae and recognizing that some of her powers have been stripped away! Immediately, the people made their way over to Zae and carried her to safety! She was injured deeply and was in agonizing pain. Zuella, could not help Zae, in any way! There were the people of Zamairria assisting Zae, having to pull out spear which was in her chest. Meanwhile, the battle of the Reyanne Kingdom and Zamairria was taking place. General Zerak, had taken Goddess Zuella to safety, and Zuella kept insisting to go back to where Zae was being treated. But General had hid Zuella with a couple of soldiers, then immediately the General left going back to the campground where the battle was taking place and commanded the people. By the time he had reached the camp, multitudes of people from both ends were falling, being killed and injured. Suddenly the air was filled with the dragons which started to shoot the fire balls, and vultures from the Kingdom of Wizerria had joined in on the battle, so it was not good for the people of Zamairria, for their Goddess was nowhere to be found because she had been restricted to help her people and her powers were restricted. So, the people of Zamairria, were losing hope since they were falling by the dozens.

Back where Goddess Zuella was at, General Zerak, had taken the Goddess to hide in the desert underground caves. While in the caves, Goddess Zuella was very worried, started to feelings of human people emotions that had the Goddess in an uproar of what was happening to her people. As the soldiers who were left to protect the Goddess started to walk further in the caves, suddenly one of the soldiers made an outburst to Zuella, "Please come and look of what I found." Speedily the Goddess, went over to look and to her surprise there was a crystalized lighting area which had the image of Goddess Zerriah, imbedded in the structure of the wall. Zuella was quite in awe, simply she had never seen this type of lighting embrace any sand or underground cave ever. As she got closer to the image carved into the wall, suddenly a beam of light shined right down upon her and the mirage of Goddess Zerriah. It appeared as it was her silhouette being shined upon her. Then as the image appeared, it introduces itself to be Goddess Zerrah, she then spoke to Goddess Zuella saying, "You have been told tales of me, and now my daughter has come into your Kingdom. I will release the powers back to you if you promise to let my daughter know whom her mother really is, and that I have always loved her and adored her. She was my true light in all that I did, unfortunately I had taken on a husband from the Kingdom of Reyvanne in lieu of believing that he could somehow love me and my daughter as his own, but as my punishment I believe it came back and surprised me. So therefore, I am truly sorry to Zae, the true heir to the Kingdom, Light of Paradise. Zae is to know exactly who she is and how much I have loved her. Plus, when she has truly found the love of her life, and that love is returned to her truly, then will she be able to sit in her place as heir to the throne, to the Light of Paradise. All this will be when you see fit to let her know, but it must be after the defeat of the Kingdom of Reyvanne. Goddess Zuella, you must let my daughter know, that I will always be with her and once she has taken her place, I will always be there for her! So be it." Goddess Zuella, then bowed her head, as she replied to her majesty, "All will be done as you requested." Zerriah, then stated to Zuella, "Return to the camp for the people of Zamairria and my daughter Zae needs you." Suddenly, Goddess Zerriah, was gone!

Chapter 17

Losing Hope

Back at the campground where the battle was taking place. General Zerak, had been ordering his troops to fight, and the people of Zamairria seemed to have been trying too, but was being outnumbered by the number of soldiers that came through from the Kingdom of Reyvanne. As the battle started to take place moving in, the creatures in the air seemed to have killed a few of the people of Zamairria. Leaving streaks of fire onto the campground. As the battle opened upon the ground and there was a passage made and straight ahead about 100 yards out, there came a huge chariot being led by tigers! It appeared to have a man with a black crown, shouting, "I am the King of Reyvanne, and we will defeat you all." This King seemed to be strong muscle bound with two swords hanging upon his side. As he proclaimed that they would defeat the people of Zamairria. Then the King then took one of his swords, and aimed it straight forward shooting out streaks of fire, lightning daggers, and killing a few people who seem to be in his way. General Zerak, then hopped on one of the stallions and rode towards, where the King of Reyvanne, road up too! He then had taken his sword, and lashed it at the King, cutting right through the King's mask, cutting him right on his face, bleeding intensely. The King then hopped off the chariot, while General Zerak jumped off the stallion so that they both can meet on ground of the battlefield and started to fight each other. Dragons and the vultures were still about and flying in air doing their share of damage to the people of Zamairria. Suddenly the battlefield seemed to get filled with bodies and bloodshed, lied on the ground. There was so much destruction being done on the battleground and the people of Zamairria started to lose faith for their fleet was now a quarter of them still standing and fighting. Without hesitation, the General looked and seen the little girl Yzelle being grabbed by the enemy and quickly started to run towards her, but to his surprise, the King of Reyvanne stuck his sword into the General's side and his sword lit up with a lightening radiation light which seem to be electrocuting the General killing him instantly. The King made a sudden shout, and laughed aloud, stating that this war is over and to all his people on ground to come see who he had slayed. During all this battling, Zae was inside a tent, where she was being attended to her wound, and she slightly looked out the tent and then heard such a beautiful voice that said, " Get up and run", she got up and started to run as if she had somewhere to go! The King's men started to shout at him, saying that "There is a lady who is running, we will go after her!" The King then replied, "No need for that, she won't be going anywhere far for there is no one left to protect her. We will catch up with her soon." Zae seemed to run into the desert and kept running till she could no longer run. She then started to sit where she had run out of breath to take a rest. Meanwhile, over at the campground the King of Reyvanne and his soldiers, seemed to be having a feast over what they so called their victory. They also had the little girl Yzelle, holding her captive. Bullying her, being cruel and scaring her. The poor little girl had seen that Zae, was nowhere to be found and started crying. The King asked her, "Why are you crying, there is no need for you will be joining all those who lost their lives today. So, don't bother, because I have no pity for any of your tears. I am the King of Reyvanne, and I will not pity anyone or any child. So, soldiers take this child out of my sight." Later, as they calm the camps down, Zae was over in the desert, trying to get rested up, and she ended up passing out in the desert! The dragons and the vultures seem to have been flying above Zae's head, but not harming her. They had a way of letting the King of Reyvanne know Zae's exact location. Truly by now, the people of Zamairria were being held captive, as well as beaten and bullied. They lost hope of anyone coming to their rescue, so it seemed to be that the people lost all hope and faith of ever being in a safe place for their lives. As the night befell, the vultures as well as the dragons, seem to have gone off away from the area. But over at the campground, the King of Reyvanne , seemed to be feasting and having no care in the world of what has just happened. All he knew was that he had conquered his so-called enemies and that he had slayed the leader of the Zamairrian people. Nothing else seemed to trouble the King's mind, but the thought of victory, embellishing in his mind. There were many other smaller chariots which had come to meet with the King of Reyvanne. Apparently, they were his people, soldiers coming to join up with him over at the campground of where the battle had taken place. They had all been celebrating the taking over of the campground where the people of Zamairria had started to set their camp. Meanwhile, the King then shouted to a few of his soldiers to come to him so that he can speak to them. "I am looking for my Commander, Reelut." This was one of his highest-ranking officers and deadly at that. So, there was King Reyvanne's soldiers scattering out to seek out his Commander named, Reelut. They searched out the Commander all over the camp and came across him upfront during their armies gathering. One of the soldiers then spotted him, and shouted out stating that "The King is needing your presence upfront immediately", then Reelut, replied, "What seems to be the problem?" The young soldier said, your presence is needed quickly." Reelut, then said, "Let's go!" and started to make his way towards the King of Reyvanne. As the Commander approached the King, the King then addressed his Commander "Set up a group to go and seek out the young lady (Zae) who had run into the desert and to kill her on sight!" The Commander stated, "Do we just kill her, or do you prefer for us to bring her back to camp so you can see her before we do away with her." The King then pondered for a few minutes, and then stated "She did look familiar, maybe that sounds better. Go ahead and capture the lady and bring her back to camp so that I may question her." The Commander then agreed to the request of King Rezeem and put his people together to start the search for Zae. There were multitudes of soldiers feasting, so then King Rezeem had called up for the little girl, Yzelle to be brought up for him to see. The soldiers then went to go and grab the girl bringing her upfront by the King, while he seemed to be boastfully arrogant about his so-called victory. It appeared as if there was no absolute resolution for the people of Zamairria. To whom all had lost their hope in anyone coming to their aide. For their leader, General Zerak, has been slayed to death. So, the people had truly lost hope in every being able to get someone to come to their rescue.

Chapter 18

A Dark King

Now that Goddess Zuella had been directed by the Halogen of Goddess Zerriah, Zuella and the soldiers had started to make their way back out of the caves in the desert. Gradually finding their way out, the Goddess then stopped and said to the soldiers, "I am feeling a bit dizzy for some apparent reason!" The Goddess then had visions as they got closer to the opening of the cave. She yelled out, "What of my people of Zamairria, what has happened?" The Goddess was starting to be able to get her gifts of vision back! It was quite disturbing for the Goddess to be able to see these visions being envisioned in her mind. She started to stand up again and shaking her head, as if she were shaking off a bad vision. Zuella, then spoke to her protectors which had watched over her, when General Zerak had left behind to protect the Goddess, she stated that "You must try their best to get back to the campground for the people of Zamairria has been slayed and the campground has been overtaken by the King of Reyvanne and all his troops. We must go at once for the people of Zamairria believe that they are alone. I cannot have my people lose faith. We must get there quickly so that they know they are not alone. I am hoping the Zae and Yzelle, plus the General are ok! For some apparent reason, I cannot tap into their feelings of emotions. There is a block in my telepathy. I cannot tap into them directly; I just feel that something awful has happen and that there is a great overwhelming sensation of fear taking over our people of Zamairria. It's almost as if there is no sense of direction being led with our people. I must go to them at once." On their journey back to the camp, Zuella had a sharp headache, and looked up to see that there seem to be a mirage, but as they continue walking it appeared to be soldiers, grabbing a lady whom appear to be Zae that was lying in the desert sand, and put her on their chariots and rode away. Zuella, seem to have been feeling a bit unusual, as if she were lightheaded. But her guards continued to push their journey. Suddenly out of nowhere, there was screeching of lightning made up of fiery bolts that lit in the sky. A raging sound of thunder and all the clouds scrolled back noticing in the air electricity bolts being shot down hitting the Goddess directly giving her a surge of energy and lighted power. She quickly fell to her knees and suddenly had such an illuminating glow about her. She then looked up, and took a deep breath, then appearing before her from out of the sky, was a white humungous eagle flying directly towards the Goddess and her protectors. Within seconds, Goddess Zerriah appeared on a mounted rock floating in the air, and began to address Goddess Zuella, "You will be taken with my Eagle, Centennial! she will safely guide you there to the camp and I will equip you with all you need to make sure that my daughter lives, and the people of Zamairria are freed and saved. Some of your powers will be restored to assist you in the battle that you will partake in at the campgrounds, where the people of Reyvanne and their King are stabilized with their fleet of soldiers. Zuella, you must seek out the three rainbow roses, that are hidden in certain Kingdoms and once these three rainbow roses, are found then will you be granted your full powers of all that you should have authority over. If touched by anyone else, the rainbow rose will wither and there will be no way of restoring your blessing powers."

While the conversation of the Goddess Zuella and Goddess Zerriah was taking place. Over at the campground, King Rezeem had ordered all his people to set out and take all their prisoners back to the Kingdom of Reyvanne, that they will depart immediately so that they can celebrate their victory on their grounds of Reyvanne. The King then looked up and seen that his Commander had road in as they were starting to depart to head back to the Kingdom of Reyvanne. The King shouts, "Great! You all joined us at a timely manner, so do you have or found the lady Zae?" The commander then replied, "We have her!" Then the King laughed loudly and said "Get all our men and grab our prisoners and head back to our Kingdom grounds of Reyvanne. We will feast today in remembrance of taking over the people of Zamairria." While the King laughed, his armies started to get all the people gathered so that they can journey back to Reyvanne. The people of Zamairria, were being taken from the campground to the Kingdom of Reyvanne, being frightened of what may occur upon their arrival. Was blatantly oblivious, that the people of Zamairria were very sadly stricken by the not knowing of any help was coming to assist them, lost with despair. Now during the time where all the people were taken, King Rezeem was quite being arrogant of the feeling being in victory. He was quite obnoxious with his behavior. So, they caravan over to the Kingdom of

Reyvanne. The desert seemed to get hot, as the caravan begun it was a couple day's travel into the desert going over to the Kingdom of Reyvanne.

Chapter 19

A Lost War

Over where Goddess Zuella and her protectors,
where they were making their way out of the desert
tunnels, again Zuella has been getting sharp pains
shooting to her head! Although this kept happening, the
protectors were adamant about pushing forward trying to
get the Goddess well, so that they can get to the
campground, where their people of Zamairria were still
being held captive by the troops of King Rezeem. Even
after the Goddess Zerriah had disappeared and that
Centennial, (the large eagle) waited for the Goddess to
come to her, there was quite a few pauses in trying to get
Goddess Zuella to proceed. As they started to go towards
Centennial, Zuella then seemed to get her footing and
started to awake in a sense of feeling a bit stronger.
While she got closer to Centennial, the Eagle had an
overwhelming beam of light shine right above her onto
her wings. Then Goddess Zuella, seen that the ray of
light on the eagle had been calling her to take a seat on
the eagles back. She then went to Centennial and her
protectors help guided the Goddess so that she was able
to get on the eagle safely! Suddenly Zuella, felt the surge
of radiance of light beaming upon her as well. At this
time rainbows of crystal sparkle made a whirlwind
around the Goddess giving her strength and taking away

her headache completely. She was being rejuvenated within the realm of lighted existence from the radiant light beaming down upon her and Centennial. One of her protectors then said, "Go on your highness, we will be shortly behind you!" So, then the eagle, (Centennial) started to expand her wings taking a couple of strokes and soon enough they were off into the beautifully deep blue sky. Their flight was very graceful, peaceful and riveting! In the air the Goddess seemed to have been able to come in touch of the illuminating light that fed her spirit and had her elevate into a higher being feeling essentially lighted from in the air. It was a flight that the Goddess needed to take, although she kept imagining her Stallion- Lightning and her in the air flying together during their times of visiting other worlds. It brought emotions of the Goddess suddenly having Zae in her mind! She had recollected the time of her first meeting with Zae and started to feel such deep emotions of the passionate kiss that they shared on one of the stallions that help her catch Zae, while falling from the air. She remembered how intense them looking into each other's eyes, and how Zae just reached over and kissed her. There were so many feelings never felt before by the Goddess herself. She could not help but think of what that all meant when Zae kissed her! But she seemed to have been put in a trans of a deep emotion filling her spirit as of a purity of love longing to be shared with her! Seemingly that flight with Centennial, was quite pleasurable and fulfilling being able to lift the Goddess's spirit to a level of much higher energy. In the skies, the rainbow sparkles seem to have followed her wherever she was flying too! As the Goddess looked over to the side suddenly, she seen a stampede of stallions flying in the air, which had joined up with her. One of the stallions flew closer to the Goddess's eagle and then caught her and stated, "Are you ok Goddess Zuella?" She then replied, "Where is Lightning? Is she around?" The stallion then said, "We thought that Lightning was with you!" She said, "I am unable to see of any of Lightnings, whereabouts! I am trying to seek out her as well as the lady Zae, and the child but I am not being successful in doing so. For some apparent reason I am still not being able to tap into some of my gifts which could pinpoint the location of certain individuals or even beings. I will continue to try and manifest my gifted powers in realms of seeking the higher energy which could help guide me to various events. I am heading back to the campground to see what has become of the people of Zamairria, Zae and the little girl named Yzelle. You all will follow me and send a few of your stallions to pick up my protectors in the sand desert that I had left behind then have them join me and your fleet of stallions over at the campground where my people of Zamairria had settled in!" The stallion, quickly responded, agreeing to what has been commanded by the Goddess Zuella, herself. As they had continued their flight, they had seen from the air, a caravan of mass amount of people being led towards the area where the Kingdom of Reyvanne, was located. But they were unable to determine what, who or what was happening down on the grounds. Goddess Zuella, stated to continue to the campgrounds of where she had commanded for them to go! As their trip was headed in the area of the campground, suddenly they looked over again towards the caravan of people and could see the coliseum of Kingdom from where they were flying! As they had been flying, there had appeared to be a huge cloud of darkness moving into the area of Kingdom of Reyvanne. Without hesitation, the clouds seem to get darker and sound of screeching seem to be heard across the land. As the Goddess continued her flight with the eagle and the stallions towards the campground they can see from the air, the dark clouds opening, with an asteroid fire ball falling from the sky, making a huge explosion shaking the grounds. From the smoke of that asteroid, appear to be as if it had opened some sort of black hole, while the caravan of people were walking about, it seemed it there was a huge ferocious creature that came out of the ground and it seemed as if people were being thrown to this creature from those riding chariots, to be eaten or killed. To the surprise of Goddess Zuella, as all this was occurring, she stayed firm to her fleet to stay on route back to the campground to find her people of Zamairria. So, continuing her flight, they were about a half a day away from the campground. Assuredly, the stallion then said, "Goddess do you think we should go over to where the caravan of people are near Kingdom of Reyvanne," but the Goddess insisted to go first to check the campgrounds to check on the people of Zamairria, not even knowing that the people that they had passed along with the caravan were actually her people from Zamairria, in which the fleet of Kingdom of Reyvanne had over taken! While moving in closer as they were getting to be able to see in sight the campground. There seem to be fires burning at the camp with tents of her people burning and there was absolutely no one in sight. It seemed to have just dead bodies laying around, that of the people of Zamairria as well as some soldiers of the Kingdom of Reyvanne. As the flight of the Goddess and her fleet of stallions started to land on ground, Zuella, then screamed a sound of a Goddess cry, knowing that those were her people, and where could Zae and Yzelle possibly be. She then walks the campgrounds, meeting with her protectors which landed shortly after the Goddess. They then took a tour of how many of the people of Zamairria had fallen, as they had come to a pit of fire burning immensely. They then seen the body of General Zerak laying in a pool of blood. The Goddess immediately order her protectors to pick up the body of General Zerak and prepare him, cleaning him and get him on a clean table so that she can see about trying to help bring his wounds to a healing. Nevertheless, the people did exactly what Zuella commanded, she then tried to seek out the gifts that she had of healing and other lighted energy vibrations, but was discouraged at not being able to tap into her gifts and not able to help her right hand protector of Zamairria, General Zerak. The Goddess was stricken with overwhelming grief for her people as well as her loyal servant, General Zerak. The Goddess then commands her protectors that they must prepare to leave immediately for the Kingdom of Reyvanne. Being stricken with the grief of not knowing where Zae & Yzelle are or even if they are still alive has made the Goddess weaken to a point of her decision makings being questionable. The outcome was farfetched of what the Goddess could even dare fathom. But it was something that she had to come to realization that the people of Zamairria, have been defeated by those whom rule their Kingdom with darkness. But knowing of who she once was, kept her will to go forth to rescue the rest of her people whether any left at all.

Chapter 20

The Death Kingdom

Back at the Kingdom of Reyvanne, King Rezeem seemed to shake his head, then shouted to some of the soldiers to "Bring forth the lady and the little girl!" Then the soldier immediately then went forth to go and grab the lady Zae and the little girl to bring in front of the King, and the King stated "Stand by the side of the lady and child while I address them. Then went on saying, "You look awfully familiar. You seem to have a familiar face. Why is it that you look as if I have known you before?" Then, Zae said, "Where do you think you know me from?" The King then replies, "You look so familiar, I believe you have a face that is of one that I know!" Zae responded, "I know of you and your destructive, cruel and killing of the innocent behaviors. I remember growing up and all the pain that you had caused to the people as well as someone who was sincerely close to me." The King then replied, "Who is this someone that was close to you?" Zae said, "That is for me to know and you try and guess, although it should not be hard at all!" The king turned his neck in an angry rage and said, "Being that you say these things of me, you need prove your accusations of me being cruel and these statements you accuse me of!" Then Zae replied, "Spare the girl I stand here with today, and you can do as you please with me!" The King said, "You will not get off that easily. So, don't bother, I will try and remember who you are then you will answer to me once I have confirmed your identity." Zae, said "In time you will find out who I really am, but by then it will have been too late for anything! All I know about you, is that you rule your Kingdom by false beliefs and torment people who are innocent. "Zae, you state that I will know sooner or later on who you are. But instead I do not care to know of who, or where you come from. I will command that my soldiers take you and have the creature take care of you for me, since this not knowing of you is useless to me period! Take this lady out of my sight and the little girl I will keep being my servant. Take this lady out of my sight and take her to the creature that awaits outside the compound of the coliseum. Therefore, await my command to take the lady but for now put her in the dungeon below so that she can have last thoughts before given to the beast creature". The dungeon that Zae had been taken too, had an underground tunnel which led outward to the compound grounds which were the outskirts of the coliseum. Now the creature whom is out of the compound wall for some reason, had an underground safety nest. The location was not to known. As the guards took Zae over to the dungeon. It was quite dark damped in the cell in which the guards had thrown her into! She yelled as they had turned their backs, "Please don't leave me here!" The guards then left, and Zae was left to await her doom! As Zae sat there in fear of her life, she then looks over to another room which she explored that had a hidden door to a what seem to be a secret pathway! As she approaches this hidden door, which was designed with skulls, vines around the edges.

Colored black with red streaks of barb wire along the hinges. Zae had no idea what was behind the door, but simply just knew that it seemed to be a secret pathway. Being that her life was on the line. She felt as if there was no opportunity for help so therefore, she must seek any way out! But in doing so, she starts to hear a gnashing sound which seemed to have a bit of a roar in the tunnel coming through the pathway! She was hesitant to try and go in any further but was reluctant and fearful! She continued into the pathway, and as she started to go further, she had discovered a dark tunnel which was lit up with skull torches, and there were multitudes of bats hanging up on wall of somewhat looking cave tunnel path! As she progressed the bats seem to have gotten larger and suddenly, she started to run! As she was running, she had noticed was a dark box looking chest with shining black and red gems on the box, she was headed towards it, but was surprised by a huge hiss and roar within the passageway. So Zae, then started to go forward and following the torches of skulls that apparently lit the cave! She traveled underground further until she came to a place and seen more light beaming from outside. She then started to follow the light shining through the cracks above the grounds. To her surprise as she got closer to the brighter light the sound of the hiss and roar became louder! Finally, down there in the passage, it became very clear how damped the passage was as well as an overpowering stench that smelled as, Zae got closer to the opening of the light. She looked straight ahead and seen all sorts of human bones lying on the ground scattered everywhere. It suddenly put her at fear with what's going on. She then analyzes whether she should continue to go forward, but then was stopped by the raging sound of the beast which was outside above the ground. She frantically came to a halt and then slightly took cover behind a door slab which was broken in half. She seemed to know that going forward could chance her to risk her life of being eaten by the creature. So, then she paused behind the door and simply waited till she had first opportunity to leave. While outside the creature had been roaming above the grounds and sounding off with hiss's and roaring while tossing human bones inside the passage underground where Zae was hiding. There were many screams of humans possibly yelling for their lives. It was sadly making Zae sick to her stomach. Although the humans were being tossed, you can also hear the stomping of a fleet of horses as well as guards. Zae could hear these things from where she was at! She was that close to hearing all the things that partook right above from where she was hiding. It was very frightful for her as well as she could not bare the stench that wreak within the passageway. Suddenly Zae heard a sound, "thump-thump" she stayed still while the sound got closer and closer. She believed the sound of the thump to be the creature, possibly getting closer to her as if it were heading her way to come back into the passageway. She then tried to look for another way out and recalled the black chest she had passed on her way out. So, then she back tracked while the sound of the thump got closer and closer. Suddenly a loud sound plundering down into the passage tunnel, she then stood to the side not trying to be seen by the creature and tried to get the black chest open so that she can hide in there. It was quite huge, she kept trying and finally the chest was able to open, and she jumped right in before the creature could notice her there. Above the ground the soldiers of Reyvanne were scattered about getting the people of Zamairria whom had gotten away from the beastly creature. There were probably hundreds of people of Zamairria, running for their lives, but was captured by the soldiers of Reyvanne. The people of Zamairria were gathered together and roped up together forming a long line, to be taken to the coliseum where King Rezeem awaited their arrival. There were hundreds of soldiers from the people of Zamairria being beaten while captured and tied up along a very extended rope tying them together as the soldiers get them ready to be taken to the grounds where the King of Reyvanne awaits their arrival. The people seem to be very challenged and had no hope in being save. They had known that they were headed to their deaths. Not one seems to have any fighting spirit left within themselves. The journey back to the Coliseum was roughly was about a day being that there was still a mass amount of people from Zamairria left. The gathering and trying to get them altogether had taken most of the day. Soldiers from Reyvanne were very brutal in their tactics towards the people of Zamairria. They traveled in the hot desert, but it started to fall into the late afternoon. As the people were taken to away from the cave where the beast had gone underground, the people of Zamairria were still fearful of at any time the beast creature could come above ground again for them. The leader of the soldiers, Commander Rezulut, had stated to his men, "Hurry get all the people of Zamairria ready for journey back to the Kingdom of Reyvanne. The King is waiting their arrival and what the beast did not get rid of, the King will determine their fate."

Chapter 21

Let the Battle Begin

Goddess Zuella, and her people were few over at the campground where the battle had taken place and her people were taken captive. She stated to the few that were with her, "We must go into the Kingdom of Reyvanne, to see what has become of the people of Zamairria." Zuella, then realized that the eagle (Centennial) which was given to her by Goddess Zerriah was only of one major help for her. The stallions were nowhere to be found. But Zuella stated "We must head over to the Kingdom of Reyvanne to seek out the people of Zamairria!" she was very concerned on what the situation was for her people. She did not quite understand or know what has happen to all her people who had been left at the campgrounds. So therefore, the people of Zamairria whom was already there with her, ended up clearing up the area and getting General Zerak's body to lay on a table which they had built and covered him, while they prepare for their journey to the grounds of Reyvanne, suddenly swirl of whirlwinds of sands started to gather blowing dust within the air, which Goddess Zuella had no control of the winds of sand at this time, plus plundering of thunders roared up in the skies as if the Goddess's were not pleased! During the duration of preparation for the journey, Goddess Zuella, then asked,

"Please give me some time" and in doing so she had gone over to a shaded spot where her people had built a tent. She pondered for some time, seeking her higher energy light to give her a sense of relief, but for some reason apparently, she was not having any type of influence from lighted energy response to her beckoning. Zuella seemed to be discouraged. But not allowing her followers, which were about 20 left there with her. She still made sure that her people did not see her discouragement towards the lack of manpower, as well as being able to tap into her powers of she had before, although she had some of her gifts, that was not going to be enough to up go up against King Rezeem and his troops. She also recalled on their journey to the camp there was a beastly creature devouring people or at least frightening them. These were the worries that Goddess Zuella endured while alone by the tent, wondering how it is going to turn out as she goes into the Kingdom of Reyvanne, unprepared for any assisting of her people that she felt were being held captive. What was she to do but go no matter the consequences, she must try and obtain her people or die trying? This weighed heavily in the Goddess's heart. Though she knew the people of Zamairria a to be outnumbered, she still insisted to go and find Zae & Yzelle and all her people left behind. Totally against all odds, it appears ever so clearly to the Goddess, that this journey must happen quickly for she has no idea on the fate of her people. Soon enough, she states to one of her protectors, "Align all who are left, then prepare for the journey to the Kingdom of Reyvanne." Sure, enough the protectors are ready to journey with their Goddess, showing their loyalty although fearful of their own lives. They stayed faithful to the Goddess, Leader of Zamairria. Now the journey has begun, still gusting of major sandstorms of whirlwinds gathering around making this journey to be very difficult. Being that the thunders in the sky roared loudly, it put some uneasy feeling within the heart of the Goddess. She knew that being that Centennial, was a large eagle it would be quite difficult for her to fly with all the sandstorms blowing ferociously about. Giving no clear passage towards the Kingdom of Reyvanne. Suddenly stallions started to make their way through the desert sandstorms bringing them in by a dozen, mounting up to at least three dozen, in which then Zuella was quite surprised. When landed the red stallion named "Zuered" went straight over to the Goddess and stated "We happen to get away during the battle over here from the campground, and as the troops of Reyvanne started killing our people I commanded the fleet of stallions to try and fly away and that we will see whether or not to come back and grab our people of Zamairria, but on our way back there was no one living to take back to our Kingdom of Zamairria. We had gone back, to be greeted over with the elders of Zamairria and the tree children in hopes of finding you there somehow. But that was not the case. Then we conferenced on seeing about trying once again if there would be any sign of our people back here at the battle ground and to our surprise, we came across you, our Goddess of Zamairria." Zuella, then stated to Zuered, "Very well, I am pleased with the notion of having leaders such as you! Thank you for not giving up and your loyalty will not be forgotten." Goddess Zuella, stated to Zuered, the fleet of stallions as well as her protectors, "This journey must happen, I am not concerned with anything but just trying to make it to the Kingdom of Reyvanne to see what is going on with my own people of Zamairria, I cannot have them lose faith in light and energy, for the greater of the good is at stake. So, let's journey with one thing in mind, whether life or death, my people of Zamairria will fight to the end. Knowing that our light shall conquer darkness somehow!" They journeyed into the desert sand storming with massive gusting of the winds, in which Goddess Zuella, had no control over. They went through the sands rugged, and Zuella, with Centennial and the troop of stallions started to travel through the rough winds of sands. The clarity was slim to none and they did the best they could in the air and continued until the coliseum was finally in view! Goddess Zuella then said, "We must land directly into the coliseum where the opening is and do not lose faith, for I believe that our higher elders somehow will be with us." Gallantly riding, the stallions which had the protectors riding with them had brought themselves forward to be at the side of their Goddess. Riding through the air the eagle, Centennial was courageous allowing the Goddess to know that she would be secure. Along the way down, she mentioned to the Goddess, "In all that you guys do, you must remember the things of Goddess Zerriah mentioned to you! But have courage for you have not gained much of the higher powers that were once yours." Zuella, then said, "I must see that Zae is alive, and all my people be brought to safety. This is going to be a battle that I will never forget since many of my people are dead and even being held captive, to a King who shows no mercy for anyone or anything! I am very concerned for my people of Zamairria, and if you should know, I am quite eager to see that the little girl named Yzelle is with the lady name Zae. I hope all is well!" Entering the grounds of Reyvanne into the coliseum, Zuella lands.

Chapter 22

The Goddess Legion

Upon the landing, immediately arrows were being shot into the air at Zuella and her fleet, injuring some. King Rezeem stood above his chair in the coliseum and laughed a wicked laugh! Seeing that the King was not in any distress upon the arrival of Goddess Zuella. Suddenly the Goddess got off the eagle with her protectors, and immediately the soldiers of King Rezeem started battling with the Goddess's people while grabbing her and bringing her upfront to the King. Her people were battling while the Goddess could do nothing, being tied up in front of the King to watch her people being slayed. The Goddess, then screamed and asked the King "Let my people go, and I will surrender to you if you allow them to live." The King stated, "I have something that may belong to you" so then the guards showed the King the little girl named Yzelle, and the Goddess shouted to the King to "Please, spare the child!" Zuella asked the King, "Where are my people of Zamairria and the lady named Zae, whom was upon my peoples care over at the campground where you had battled my people and held them captive." The King then laughed obnoxiously and said "Half of your people are being held in our dungeons and the rest are dead. Plus, the lady, I believe you talk about, my soldiers will bring her forth now." During the captivity of the Goddess, it appeared she was losing faith. Suddenly, the King's soldiers ran out saying that the Zae escaped, they cannot find any sign of the Zae anywhere. The King did not seem to be laughing anymore, he became furious and sent out three quarters of his army to search out for Zae. The soldier of the King went high and low in search of Zae, they ended up going to the place where Zae was held captive and noticed the same passage which Zae had come across, and to their surprise she had been hiding out in the passageway, which led them to the beastly creature's dungeon. Upon them stumbling throughout the passage they came across the black chest and seen that Zae was there behind the broken door, they immediately grabbed her in hopes not to alarm the beastly creature which looks as a dragon with bat like wings and sharp gnashing teeth, whom has the ability to shoot out venom which will kills instantly. The guard's, soldiers of Reyvanne then took her to the King. While the King laughed again louder, he noticed that Zuella had placed her head down, then he told her, "You might want to look up as I question, this lady on who she is!" Zae, then was drugged to the feet of the King and thrown there. Zae looked up and noticed that there stood Goddess Zuella, they then locked eyes for quite some time. Zae was a bit relieved but still at the same time was fearful of the unknowing of may take place. The King then addressed, Goddess Zuella, and stated "You cannot have Zae, but could take the little girl named Yzelle and you can go free, but the people of Zamairria will serve me under my Kingdom. Goddess Zuella then replied, "That will not happen" Soon enough they heard screeching, roaring of the beastly creature as if it were making its way through the coliseum! Suddenly the people of Zamairria were all brought to the coliseum to be shown to the Goddess of how many survived. There were still hundreds of the people of Zamairria being brought forth for the Goddess to view, while Zae was at the feet of the King of Reyvanne. The Goddess then implied "I cannot go and leave my people here in this Kingdom. So, then the Goddess, screamed a loud scream to the King, uttering "You are such a wicked soul; how can you do this to people whom are innocent!" While laughing with arrogance the King then stated "Whom are you to judge me? I am King Rezeem, you go now or never!" Goddess Zuella then turned to take the child Yzelle into her hands and comforted and said to the King "I will be back for my people!" As Goddess Zuella turned around to start walking towards the eagle, Centennial, which stood at the center of the coliseum. The King grabbed onto to his sword, made of the black, chrome plated with skulls and red ruby gems aligned with his blade. The handle had a piercing crystal which inside was a rainbow color rose imbedded in the gem. Although it seems hard to get a good view on exactly what color was the rose imbedded in the gem at the handle of the sword. It seems to have rainbow looking color that gleamed through the gem. Suddenly as the Goddess turned her back, King Rezeem reached for his sword and pulled it out and plunged it towards the Goddess intending to stab her, but immediately Zae stood up and placed her body to shield Goddess Zuella. The sword pierced right through Zae's abdomen, bringing her to her feet! Goddess Zuella, turned back quickly to see the sight of Zae falling to her feet with the sword pierced in her, slowing falling to the ground, Zae caught Goddess Zuella's eyes with a look of admiration of love for her. Zuella stricken with immense grief, while King Rezeem seemed to be laughing. This made Zuella, extremely sadden and heart broken, leaving one tear drop falling from her right eye. Behold, Zae had fallen, while the tear dropped from Goddess Zuella's eyes it did not even reach the bottom of her face, suddenly a bolt of lightning jolted from the sky. Extreme loud sounds roaring of thunders, dark clouds rolling back and to the right of the sky appeared an opening with clouds shaped as door right in the sky with a beaming, glittering light, and before them all appeared a legion of Goddess's dress with crystalized warrior dress with swords designed light lightning bolts. This door entrance opened for the Legion of Goddess's to come through. The King and Goddess Zuella in awe of what is currently taking place. The Goddess's in the sky were in the numbers, wearing their crowns and bracelets of rainbow gold with bolts attached to them. They all had a protective wall around them beaming with extreme brightness. Then as the stood from the clouds, a rainbow color ball came to the forefront and opened with Goddess Zerriah, standing with chrome color, gown wearing a Goddess crown designed out of the world. Goddess Zerriah, then spoke, and her voice carried throughout, she addressed the King and stated "I am here for my daughter, Zae." The King said, "I know of you, I will kill you again as I did the first time, but this time I will feed you to my beastly creature." As the King was addressing the Goddess the Creature was being let loose from the bottom to roam the grounds of Reyvanne. By then, the Goddess's were descending on the grounds of Reyvanne, ready for battle. As the Legion of Goddess's were touching ground, they were being attack immediately by the soldiers of Reyvanne and the Goddess's were fighting with their swords and the bolted rainbow bracelets shooting bolts and killing the soldier guards of Reyvanne. The soldiers of Reyvanne were fighting but were no match for the Legion of Goddess's. Goddess Zuella seemed to have ascended to the Goddess's side, while Goddess Zerriah came from the sky and landed onto the ground. By then the beastly creature had made its way to the outskirts of the coliseum. The soldiers of Reyvanne were aligning for battle but could not overpower the Goddess Legion, suddenly the voice of Goddess Zerriah, stated "Surrender the people of Zamairria over, or this will not end well for you, King Rezeem and your Kingdom." The King arrogantly laughed, "There is no way!" As Goddess Zerriah looked down, she seen the body of Zae, and then suddenly the soldiers of Reyvanne began attacking more diligently but was very unsuccessful trying to defeat the Goddess's. The battle continued with the people of Zamairria, the lighted Goddess's, against the beastly creature and the entire region of Reyvanne. Goddess Zerriah, looked down at her daughter, Zae and as she looked over to Goddess Zuella, she then noticed that Zuella was crying over the body of her daughter Zae, and right there, the sky shot a ray of bright beam upon her daughter Zae's body, and the sword of the King was being removed by this extreme bright crystalized light, suddenly the wounds of Zae were healed up, and she came to life, transforming into the rightful heir to her mother, Goddess Zerriah. Goddess Zuella's was surprise, the sword that took Zae's life was afloat in the air, waiting upon the hand of Zae, to take it! As Zae transformed, she had a bright fiery red garment with lightning bolts with a prince crown on, immediately Zae took the sword and smashed the blade to the ground cracking the gem, allowing the rainbow rose to come forth and to be imbedded in the prince crown right above her head, Zae was immediately crowned her status from the Goddess Zerriah. The beastly creature had made its way into the coliseum killing the people of Zamairria making its way directly towards Zae, the beast the lashed out towards Zae, then Zae reached for the sword above her head and pierced it directly into the beast's head killing it instantly. While surprised the King looked at Zae, and uttered to her, "Now I remember you, you are the child that my Queen had bare. Zae then replied, "Your world of darkness is no more!" then Goddess Zuella looked at Zae, dropping one tear for her love that she had for Zae, then suddenly a beam of lightning bolts hit Zae, empowering her with all her powers over the world. Suddenly out of nowhere the stallions appeared and the people of Zamairria were taken, to free them, while Goddess Zuella, looked towards the Goddess Zerriah, Zerriah stated "Now has come for you two to spread the unity of light and energy throughout." Soon enough the King laughed and said, "There is no getting rid of me. Zerriah, then said to Zae, "I have always loved you my child. I have extended your powers to you, Goddess Zuella, you must seek out the two other rainbow roses for all your powers to be given back! You still have command of the waters and again the grounds, and sand. We will depart from you now, Zae!! remember I am always with you!" The battle of the grounds had completely stopped, and Goddess Zuella said to Zae "May I look at your crown" during the things which were being displayed right in front of the King. Then King

Rezeem stated to the Goddess and Zae that you guys will not get too far. That remains to be seen, as Zae reached for her crown, she handed it over to Zuella and the Goddess, touched the crown where the rainbow rose was imbedded and suddenly the rose came out of the gem, and appeared to be a live rainbow rose in Goddess Zuella's hands. Zuella, had a huge smile, and then said to all that she commanded to journey with her back to the Kingdom of Zamairria, as they all gathered to depart. The King arrogantly said, "This is not over!!" Goddess Zuella, then said, follow me and as the people of Zamairria departed, Goddess Zuella, and Zae led the people out, and at the same time, the waters and sand screens, came through without touching the people of Zamairria, and destroyed all that was not good. The waters flooded the Kingdom of Reyvanne, while the King had done something of darkness and as he spoke to the grounds it had open a dark hole into a realm of darkness opening a black hole, the King and some of his people entered before the waters consumed everything and the people of Reyvanne that weren't able to go through the black hole. Zuella and Zae rode away together heading back to the Kingdom of Zamairria, but as they journey Zae was hit suddenly with a bolt of dark lightning making her dizzy falling off the eagle and as she fell into the sky, memories of flashes of her life befell her. She had flashes of whom her mother was and the world of lighted beings. The flashes were strong as she was falling, but then was caught again in the midst of the air by her Goddess Zuella, with the eagle Centennial. Zae then was in the hands of Zuella again. They looked at each other flying in the air and suddenly Zae kissed Zuella stating, I believe I am in love with you. Still shaking her head while flashes still were playing in her head. They ended up flying coming to the campground where the battle first started with their fleet of stallion and their people in preparing of heading back to their grounds of the Kingdom of Zamairria. Zae ended up just holding Zuella and kissing her while on their journey with constant flash backs of the lighted Kingdom realm that she remembered of her mother, Goddess Zerriah! She then said, to Goddess Zuella, "I am remembering the higher lighted realm where my mother had come from. It is a beautiful realm filled with nothing but love surrounding all the legions." Zuella, then reaches for Zae and holds her tight, then kisses her again while in flight with Centennial. The continue their journey together falling for one another deeply. Being mesmerized by the love that is within them together for each other.

A word about the author...

My name is Barbara Falo aka RainowPrince. I am from sunny San Diego, California, born and raised. There is not much that I don't enjoy! I am kind, respectful, and very people oriented. I enjoy a great game of pool, and recently explored my writing skills again. I am passionate about putting down the depths of how I feel into a book. I am very optimistic and usually understanding. I love helping people, but the great joy is being married to my wife, as well as having our four kids. God is the sole reason for all my creative writing, and of course, my wife and children play a great part in my inspiration. They have been very motivational; I have always believed in loving outside the box. Meaning loving others, then those you are supposed to! I am an individual that believes in no matter who you are, and if needed help, I am there if situations permit! Our family solely strives in sharing that God is Great all day, every day! At this time, I have taken time to explore what I have always enjoyed doing which is writing.

www.rainbowprincewritings.com

www.ingramcontent.com/pod-product-compliance
Lightning Source LLC
Chambersburg PA
CBHW071406170626
46811CB00003B/1273